AMONG THE RIVER PIRATES

Hugh Lloyd

Pharos Books

ISBN: 978-93-55462-04-6
eISBN: 978-93-55462-12-1

©Publisher

Publisher: Pharos Books (P) Ltd.
Plot No.-63, 1st Floor, Main Mother Dairy Road
Pandav Nagar, East Delhi-110092
Phone: 011-40395855, +4049916623
WhatsApp: +91 9319228272
E-mail: sales@pharosbooks.in
Website: www.pharosbooks.in
First Edition: 2024

AMONG THE RIVER PIRATES
Hugh Lloyd

CONTENTS

CHAPTER I

UPSTREAM

The shabby old motor boat moved slowly up the river towing an equally shabby old barge. Dilapidated and unpainted as the hull was, the engine was well muffled—suspiciously well muffled—and the disreputable looking craft moved through the water with all the noiseless dignity of a yacht.

A ferry-boat paused midway of the long tow rope and its commuters, crowded on the forward deck, watched this slow-moving procession with some show of annoyance. Not a few impatient remarks rose loud and clear above the hum of the restless crowd, directed at the head of a man seated in the stern of the boat, calmly puffing on a pipe. Aft on the barge, a young boy was wrestling heroically with the tiller, trying to keep the lumbering hulk head on.

Slowly they crawled upstream. On their left was the precipitous Jersey shore, and on their right the towering buildings of the great city. Over the water the late afternoon sun spread a warm, mellow glow and touched with gold the myriad windows of the clustering skyscrapers across the river.

The man knocked out his pipe with calm deliberation and turned his wide, gray eyes to the lofty Palisades, now bathed in a dazzling crimson. Then slowly his glance wandered back to where the shimmering light fell across the little shanty on the barge and picked out in hold relief the incongruously new and shining letters, *Minnie M. Baxter.*

A smile lighted up his lined, weary features, a smile of pride in ownership.

"She ain't so bad fer the old battle-axe that she is, hey Skippy?" he called to the boy.

The boy's tousled head appeared from around the battered cabin.

"I'll say she ain't, Pop," he answered. "An' she's *ours!* Gee, I can't believe my pop really an' truly owns a *whole* barge!"

The man laughed, then listened for a moment to a significant sound emanating from the muffled engine.

"That there front cylinder's missin' agin, Skippy," he shouted. "Loop 'er in that there ring; the tide's runnin' out now so she'll stand upstream. Set 'er even 'n' come aboard here."

The boy nodded obediently and with an end of rope fastened the old tiller to a rusty ring. Then, hurrying forward, he jumped into the water and grasping the taut tow line, pulled himself hand over hand and scrambled over the stern of the launch.

The father put out a large, work-worn hand and helped him in with a tenderness that was surprising in one so rough and uncouth looking.

"Gimme that there shirt and them shoes while I hang 'em near the engine," he said, his voice soft with affection. "Ye'll be gettin' a bad throat agin." He made no demand for the boy's trousers, which were the only other article of apparel that the little fellow wore.

Having spread the clothing to dry and adjusted the rebellious motor, the man returned to the stern. He relighted his pipe and sat down with an arm about his son.

"I'll steer her fer a while, Pop," said Skippy.

For a few minutes there was silence.

"Yer glad we're goin' straight?" the man asked with a sudden move of his arm on the boy's shoulder.

Skippy's eyes widened and he looked up at his parent, hesitantly.

"I mean yer glad we're goin' straight—in a straight racket, I mean? Now there ain't goin' to be no more worry about coppers. I won't care if they're floatin' all over the harbor an' I won't be worryin' about no pinches. A man don't ever think uv bein' pinched when his racket's on the up and up. An' that's me from now on. I said when I got three hunderd saved I'd buy a barge an' not touch no more shady rackets. *An' I have!* Three hunderd—every penny we had in the world, sonny, I paid Josiah Flint fer the *Minnie M. Baxter.* She's worth every dime uv it."

Skippy nodded gravely.

"An'll that help me t' be honest when I grow up, too," he asked eagerly, "an' be like—like a gentleman even?"

"Sure, Skippy. Ain't that just why I saves up an' buys the *Minnie M. Baxter?* So's yer kin grow up clean an' honest like—that's why I done Josiah Flint's dirty work fer his dirty money! So's I could save an' buy this ol' battle-axe an' give yer a good an' a clean start."

"But we're gonna carry garbage an' ashes on her," said Skippy. "That ain't so clean exactly, is it, Pop?"

"Garbage an' ashes'll bring in clean money, Skippy—that's what I'm talkin' about—clean money. Since yer ma died I ain't had many real honest like jobs. It's been hard ter git 'em with yer needin' me with yer so much counta yer bad throat. Anyways the money come easier an' quicker on my jobs even if it was dirty an' now I'm all through with gettin' it shady like."

"An' my throat's lots better'n it usta be, Pop," said Skippy eagerly. "I ain't had a bad one for three months'n over."

"Sure, I know. Everthin'll be jake now with us goin' straight. Ol' Flint, let him have his dirty money an' his fine yacht. It's a wonder he gets so generous an' sells me such a good scow fer three hunderd smackers. Everybody says he's such a money-pincher he'd even try makin' money on a rusty nail."

"A regular miser, huh, Pop?" said Skippy. "Maybe he felt sorry about you savin' all that money so's you could get a clean business. Did he say the *Minnie M. Baxter's* a good barge for haulin' garbage an' ashes?"

"Sure. He boosted her hisself when I tells him I wants a good scow. An' he oughta know, him that owns more scows'n he can count."

"Gee, three hunnerd dollars—real money," mused the boy.

"Sure, but not for no scow like this one. Brand new ones cost four times that. Big Joe Tully paid Ol' Flint five hunderd fer his an' Joe cleaned up two thousand bucks on the first year. He tole me that fer a fact."

"But ain't Big Joe Tully doin' sumpin' for Mr. Flint now?" Skippy asked.

"Big Joe can't keep away from dirty money," replied the man. "He wants to get rich quick. Not me, though. I can keep away from Ol' Flint from now on, an' what's more, *I will*!"

"Gee, I know you will, Pop," said the boy, with shining eyes. "You're not like—well, you're different from old Mr. Flint an' that Big Joe."

The father ran his hand over his son's tousled head and gripped a handful of the straight brown hair affectionately.

"That cabin ain't goin' ter make us no bad little shack, hey Skippy?" he said nodding toward the little square shelter aft.

"She's swell inside—for a barge, I mean. Three bunks an' a nice oil stove an' a table an' chairs. Gee, that's a regular home, huh Pop? Even there's a kerosene lamp."

"Sure. Yer can read books an' be nice and comfortable in there nights. That paint job," he said, scrutinizing it thoughtfully; "I ain't so fond uv that there red, rusty color. It's kinda gloomy. Well, we can repaint her sometime when we're makin' money. Blamed if that launch across stream ain't headin' straight this way."

"It's the harbor inspectors, Pop. Whadja s'pose...."

"Well, I got my license all ready, if that's what they're after. Anyways, we ain't got no stuff[1] aboard, so we should worry."

Skippy wondered and shivered a little. His father's services in the employ of the rich, unscrupulous Josiah Flint had brought a certain instinctive fear of all uniformed officials and the harbor inspectors were no exception. It was difficult for him to believe even now that these uniformed men meant no harm to his father.

Skippy had lived in the shadow of the law a little too long.

***

CHAPTER II

CONDEMNED

Skippy watched as the green, shining launch swept alongside and stopped. He was instantly reassured, however, when its occupants smiled genially at him and then at his father.

"Well, if it ain't Toby Dare himself," said one of the men, heartily. "Buy her lately, Dare?"

"Jes' yesterday, Inspector Jones," said Skippy's father, proudly. "An' I ain't a-goin' ter put nothin' on her but what I'll be glad ter show ter anybody what asks."

Inspector Jones' bland face became serious.

"Big Joe Tully said the same thing when he bought his scow, Dare," he said. "I wouldn't make promises too soon."

Toby Dare's eyes turned fondly on his son.

"Big Joe Tully ain't got no boy like my Skippy ter fetch up," he said with firm resolve.

"Good for you, Dare," the inspector smiled. "Skippy's worth keeping out of trouble for. But see that you keep him in mind when you're tempted. Most o' you birds that start a new leaf stub your toes."

"Not me," said Toby vehemently. "I ain't carin' ter make no quick fortune. A couple grand a year'll start Skippy an' git him educated. That's all I'm carin' about, Inspector. *Me*, I don't need nothin'."

Inspector Jones beamed upon the smiling Skippy, then casually glanced toward the barge.

"*Minnie M. Baxter*, eh?" he mused.

"Yere," said Toby exultantly. "That was my wife's name when she was a girl. She died when Skippy was born. I thought mebbe the name'd bring me luck."

The inspector nodded sympathetically.

"Got any contracts lined up?" he asked.

"Two," said Toby proudly. "An' it ain't bad fer a start. I'm ter haul garbage an' ashes from the island."

"Good for you, Dare. Well, we'll look her over and pass on her, then let you beat it."

Toby Dare looked exultantly at his son as the trim green launch chugged off to circle the barge. It was a look of triumph and of high hopes for the future.

"All we need's his O.K., Skippy," he said in soft tones. "It's somethin' ter be able ter face guys like the inspector, specially when I been dodgin' him so long."

"Then he knows you usta——" Skippy's tongue seemed not to be able to say the word.

"Sure," said Toby, a little abashed. "There ain't many reg'lars in this harbor that the inspector ain't got spotted some time or other. But I should worry now."

Skippy nodded happily and a silence ensued between them. They listened together and watched while the harbor launch paused midway of the *Minnie M. Baxter* and Inspector Jones and his two subordinates held an inaudible conference. Then for a time they made soundings after which the inspector boarded the barge and spent another five minutes inspecting it fore and aft.

"There's more ter this here inspectin' business than what a guy thinks," said Toby simply. "All I know uv boats is this here kicker. I never did more'n load an' unload aboard Ol' Flint's scows."

"The inspector's gettin' back in the launch," said Skippy eagerly. "Now they'll come back an' say it's all right an' then we can go, huh?"

Toby Dare nodded and smilingly waited as the launch chugged back alongside of his kicker.

"What yer think uv my ol' battle-axe, hey, Inspector?" he asked, chuckling.

"Battle-axe is a good word for her, Dare," said the inspector solemnly. "Nothing describes her better."

Toby Dare's generous mouth seemed to tighten at the corners.

"What yer mean, Inspector?"

"How much did you pay for her?"

"Three hunderd—why?" Toby's lips trembled a little and he searched the inspector's face anxiously.

"Who'd you buy her from?" the inspector persisted.

"Ol' Flint! Josiah Flint," Toby answered suspiciously. "*Why?*"

"I thought it must be somebody like him. I hate to spring it on you, Dare, but you've paid three hundred dollars too much. She's not worth a dime."

Toby Dare cleared his throat and a strange look came into his kindly gray eyes.

"Inspector ——, yer mean this here barge ain't...." he began.

"She's not seaworthy," the inspector interposed as kindly as he could. "It's not safe to keep her afloat, Dare. Flint gypped you. You should have had somebody look her over before you bought her— somebody that knew an up-and-coming barge from driftwood. That's all you got on your hands, I'm sorry to say—*driftwood*. Her keel's as rotten as a keel can possibly be."

Toby Dare's tanned, weather-beaten face went suddenly white and he made a funny little clicking noise with his tongue.

"The keel," he muttered hoarsely, "can't I have 'er fixed, Inspector— *can't I?*"

Inspector Jones shook his head.

"It'd take more money than what you paid for the old hulk, Dare; more money than you've got, I guess."

"I ain't got a cent, Inspector, that's the truth," Toby said, choking on his words. "Every cent I had I paid Ol' Flint an'—an'...."

Inspector Jones leaned toward the miserable man.

"Don't take on so, Dare. Maybe the thing's not as hopeless as it seems. If Josiah Flint's got a spark of human feeling he'll make good. Perhaps he didn't realize what shape the barge was in when he sold her. He owns so many...."

"That's jest it, Inspector," said Toby, clenching his calloused hands. "Ol' Flint *ain't* got human feelin'. I worked fer him an' I know. An' fer a big ship-owner like him, he knows every craft he owns like a book. Now that I think uv it, I know he knew what he was sellin' me! He knew I was dumb about them things an' he took advantage uv it." Dare looked down the harbor, glowing in the sunset, and his jaw was set determinedly. "He smiled, Ol' Flint did, when I forked over my jack. He knew all the time!"

Skippy's eyes were misty and he looked appealingly at Inspector Jones.

"Does that mean Pop can't use the *Minnie M. Baxter*?" he faltered.

The inspector averted his face from the boy's pleading eyes.

"If you think you can't appeal to Flint personally, Dare," said he, "sue him. A lawyer'll make him kick in."

"Not from Ol' Flint," said Toby Dare hoarsely and looking straight across the river. "He's too rich ter be sued. But there's one way uv fixin' him—*one way*!"

Inspector Jones motioned his men to start their craft on its way.

"Cheer up," he said, glancing quickly from father to son. "You'll get a break yet. The safest way to get after Flint, Toby, is to sue him. You'd certainly not get anywhere with him the way you feel now. Meanwhile, the safest place for the scow is up at the Basin. She's just not safe even to be towed around the harbor."

Skippy watched the long line of foam that the launch left in its wake. For a long time his misty eyes were fastened on the glistening bubbles dancing atop the water until he could no longer stand his father's silence.

"Pop, Pop," he stammered, "can't we go—go somewhere now?"

"Sure—sure," said Toby brokenly. "We're goin' somewheres a'right. We're goin' ter the Basin where Jones told us to go with the *Minnie M. Baxter*." He laughed sardonically. "We're goin' ter put the ol' battle-axe in dry-dock *forever*!"

"What's that mean, Pop?" Skippy asked pathetically. "It sounds like you mean something terrible will happen to the *Minnie M. Baxter*."

"It *is* terrible ter me—an' ter you, Skippy boy," mumbled Toby. "It means that the pore scow's so rotten she ain't fit fer nothin' but ter be put high an' dry in Brown's Basin along with half a hunderd other rotten scows. It's way in the inlet an' folks live in them scows like I guess you an' me'll have ter till I kin think what next."

"Then all those other barges like ours can never sail the harbor again, huh?" Skippy asked sadly. "They just sorta stay there till they rot an' fall apart, is that it? Like as if they're condemned."

"That's the word, Skippy," said Toby Dare bitterly. "The *Minnie M. Baxter's* been condemned an' you an' me are condemned along with her."

***

CHAPTER III

THE BASIN

Brown's Basin was off the beaten track, even nautically speaking. One could never have found it except by the merest chance, unless one were fortunate enough to have a companion who was familiar with it. The rivermen knew, perhaps knew too well, as did the police who preferred to get no closer to the colony than the shadowy inlet which sulks silently in the daylight hours and strangely springs to life under cover of the blackest nights.

The Basin, as it is more familiarly known, thrives under the protection of the lofty Palisades. In summer the foliage all but hides it from the shore, and in winter the grim, gray rocks give it ample security from the prying eyes of the world. And the Basin wishes that security, for the character of the residents is such that secrecy and isolation provide the means for their livelihood and their existence.

Perhaps half a hundred derelict barges dot the slimy mud banks of the Basin, some of them occupied and some not. But on the whole the combined population of this sordid looking place represents a fair number and on bright, sunlit mornings one can get an occasional glimpse from the steep river road of poorly clad children scrambling from one to the other of the closely packed barges, much the same as they would scramble across city streets.

Large planks connect the sprawling hulks in a sort of interminable chain and the denizens can traverse the entire settlement by this means. More often than not the family laundry waving in the damp river breeze on the forward deck must be dodged by this strolling citizenry, but they are quite used to all forms of adroit evasion, particularly where the law is concerned.

It was into this little lawless colony that the *Minnie M. Baxter* was towed. Sunset had long since gone, leaving but a hint of vermilion colored sky at the horizon as the kicker chugged silently farther and farther into the muddy waters of the inlet. Skippy steered the motor-boat and Toby Dare struggled at the tiller of the barge while most of the colonists looked on indifferently. They sprawled about on the various decks, men, women and children.

Criticism, both friendly and otherwise, reached Toby Dare's sensitive ears, but he paid little heed, using his own judgment as to a suitable spot in which to rest the ill-fated barge. It was a spot at the very edge of the Basin that he chose and so manifest was its isolation from the rest of the colony that but one inference could be drawn: Toby Dare did not intend his son or himself to be drawn into that maelstrom of dubious citizenry. His grief over the recent misfortune in no way blunted his keen senses and, as always, Skippy's future welfare was uppermost in his mind.

"They're people what ain't partic'lar 'bout things, Sonny," he explained while the *Minnie M. Baxter* was settling in the mud. "They— well, they can't help it, but they're folks what ain't carin' whether their boys is fetched up right or not. They jest let their kids live day after day sorta an' they don't think uv next year. Me, I'm always a-thinkin' 'bout you a year ahead—see? So it ain't no use botherin' with folks what thinks different."

"I see, Pop," said Skippy looking musingly into the rust-colored water. "You know all about 'em, huh?"

"More'n they know themselves, Sonny. Ain't they slaves fer Ol' Flint same as I was? Only I did more uv his high class dirty work. I overseed 'em load an' unload the stuff fer Ol' Flint an' it paid enough ter keep my sonny in a shack ashore where he didn't see his Pop helpin' ter beat the law. Now when I thought I was through with that an' ready ter give yer a clean, honest start—*where am I?*" He buried his face in his hands.

Skippy touched his father on the shoulder with a trembling hand.

"Aw, Pop—forget it, huh? I can help soon too, can't I? When I get my workin' papers I can. I'll even go to night school an' I'll be honest an' like a gentleman just the same as if the *Minnie M. Baxter* wasn't condemned an' we could haul garbage an' ashes an' make plenty." He was quite exhausted by this lengthy declaration but his eyes were full of shining hope.

Toby Dare raised his head.

"Yer a-meanin' well, Sonny, but yer ain't got no idea how hard it is ter do anythin' without a little money. Besides, it sort uv taints a man's own fam'ly even, when he's worked fer Ol' Flint. Decent, honest shipowners give a man the go-by when they find out yer been a Flint man. Yer blackballed, in other words, Sonny—see? Yer ain't given no chance ter work at an honest job no matter how bad yer want to. An' I can't do nothin' but river work an' the like—I ain't never done nothin' else! The only thing fer a man like me ter do was ter try an' go on his own hook like I meant ter do with the *Minnie M. Baxter.* Now I can't do that unless—unless...." His large, yellow teeth seemed to close over the word hopefully.

"Unless what, Pop?" Skippy asked eagerly.

"Unless I kin make him give me back my money an' I kin buy another *Minnie M. Baxter.*" He choked a little and shook his disheveled head. "But that's too much ter hope fer, Skippy. Ol' Flint's never been known ter give anythin' back—it's me that oughta know that. I was a fool ter think he could be honest with me—*me*, a poor workman uv his. Why, Ol' Flint's bragged he'd skin anybody what was fool enough ter *be* skinned."

Skippy shifted uncomfortably from one foot to the other.

"So then will you go to a lawyer like Inspector Jones told you? To please me, Pop, will you?"

"I'm a-goin' nowheres but ter see Ol' Flint," answered Toby hoarsely. "That swell yacht uv his is anchored in the bay an' he's livin' aboard it

Among the River Pirates

durin' this hot spell so I know where ter find him after workin' hours. He ain't only ten years older 'n me an' he's in good condition an' jest my size so...."

"Pop—Pop, you got fight on your mind an' it's just the way Inspector Jones warned you not to go to see Mr. Flint! Besides, it ain't gonna be half bad here till we can think up sumpin' else to do. Forget about Mr. Flint if you're jus' thinkin' of him on accounta me. I'll be all right—"

"I'll forget anythin' 'ceptin' that Ol' Flint's cheated me with a grin on his slick face," said Toby Dare with an ominous softness in his voice. "So I'm a-goin' ter teach him a lesson, Skippy—I'm a-goin' ter teach him that Toby Dare can't be cheated outa everythin' he's hoped fer, fer years, without hittin' back. Yessir, Ol' Flint's gotta learn what it means ter cheat me!"

"Pop—Pop! You ain't goin'—honest?"

"I am. I'm a-goin' sure as guns."

"When—when you goin', Pop?"

"*Tonight!*"

***

CHAPTER IV

COMPROMISE

Skippy got the first meal aboard the *Minnie M. Baxter*. His heart and soul were certainly not in the task for he burned four of the flapjacks that he was cooking. The coffee had twice boiled over and the narrow little cabin was filled with a blue, acrid smoke and though the sight of his father's lugubrious face, as he paced up and down outside the little windows, disturbed him, he was not particularly unhappy.

His mind, during the preparation of that meal, was not on his father's misfortunes nor on the threatened and ominous visit to the Flint yacht that very evening. Instead he was visualizing what benefits were to be derived from residing in the Basin, chief among these being an uninterrupted summer season of fishing and swimming. That to the heart of a boy of his age compensated fully for the loss of the garbage and ashes contract, yes, even for the loss of the barge's promise of a remunerative future.

It is not to be thought that Skippy did not deeply feel his father's grief, for indeed he had brooded over it for hours. But after they had settled and arranged their few belongings in the meagerly furnished cabin of the barge, he had achieved that blessed miracle of youth and accepted the inevitable without a question. Life stretched out ahead of him as the inlet lay spread under this starlit night, broken now and then by a quiet ripple until it reached the river. What would happen beyond that point he knew he could find out when he came to it.

And so, more contented than his brooding and troubled parent, Skippy piled up the flapjacks until they resembled the leaning tower of Pisa, and he whistled to the accompaniment of the sputtering coffee pot. All the world seemed delightful and generous with these savory dishes ready to be eaten, and he asked himself if his father wasn't making much of little. After all, they had the *Minnie M. Baxter* for a home, didn't they? And wasn't living on a barge just the kind of life that he and his pals had often wished for when they had lain about their dusty dooryards on hot summer nights?

The boy ran to the door, his tanned face flushed and expectant. He would tell his father how much better he was going to feel out on the river all summer than back in dusty, hot Riverboro where he had spent all his life. He would fish and swim and take lots of deep, lung-developing breaths. He'd probably never have another bad throat....

He inhaled deeply on the strength of this thought and though his lungs filled with a queerly mixed odor of mud, decayed fish and salt, he noticed it not at all. Moreover, the inlet might have been a clear, wind-swept ocean waste, so far above the Basin had his imagination carried him.

A figure stirred in the shadows forward and then he heard the familiar tread of his father. Suddenly on the damp salt breeze they heard the distant sound of chimes and waited silently while the faint notes struck off the hour of ten.

"Pretty late to eat, huh Pop? Everythin's ready, so you better come while it's hot."

"Yer know where them chimes come from?" Toby asked in a tone of voice that was strange to his son. "They come from River Heights on that swell Town Hall what Ol' Flint give to the borough. Now I s'pose he'll give the three hunderd dollars he cheated me outa, fer somethin' else what'll give him a big name, hey? That's what some uv them scoundrels like Ol' Flint do—give their dirty money ter things what'll give 'em a fine big name. Well, he won't git the chanct ter give my three hunderd—not while I live!"

Josiah Flint again! Skippy's heart lost all its merry hopes in a fleeting second. He turned back into the cabin and his father followed him in gloomy silence. Mechanically, he carried the steaming plate from the oil stove to the rickety little oil-cloth covered table and without a word they pulled up their chairs and sat down.

"I never tole yer before," said Toby after a few moments, "but if it wasn't fer Ol' Flint there wouldn' never 'a' been no squatter colony like this in Brown's Basin. It's him what's made it, that's what. They're all blackballed men, Sonny; men what's got in Ol' Flint's clutches an' ain't never got the chance nor the brains ter git out. Not like me that had a little more brains ter earn bigger money so's I could save fer the *Minnie M. Baxter. Save!*" He brought his fist down upon the table with such force that a flapjack bounced from his plate to the floor. "Ha, ha—what for did I save, hey?"

He laughed so sardonically that Skippy hurried for the coffee to hide his concern.

"Aw, please don't take on so, Pop!" His eyes were directed at Toby's back. "Gee, that old miser, he ain't worth you actin' so queer an' all. It ain't so bad here. It's a nice little house we got in this cabin; chairs an' the stove an' a table an' our trunk." His glance wandered to the tiny windows opened to the damp salt breeze. "Even I bet I could put up some cretonne stuff as good as a girl an' then won't this be one nice-lookin' little place!"

Toby's chair scraped over the rough, clean boards and he stood up, straight and powerful and ominous.

"Never mind the coffee now," he said hoarsely. "We kin heat it up an' drink it when we come back." He laughed. "We'll drink it as a toast ter Ol' Flint's health!"

Skippy put down the coffee pot and wiped his grimy hands on his khaki knickers. Then with a swift movement he shook back his straight, rebellious hair and glanced up at his father.

"You—you mean you want me with you, Pop?" he asked tremulously.

"*Jest* what I mean, Skippy. I want yer along so's I kin remember Ol' Flint ain't worth ... well, what I mean is, if I have yer to talk ter on the way I ain't so like ter lose my head when I git there an' talk ter him. If he gits sneerin' at me like his habit is mostly, it'll be good fer me ter know my Sonny's right outside a-waitin' in the kicker. Waitin' fer his Pop, hey?"

Among the River Pirates

"Sure, sure," Skippy gulped. "Sure, I'll go with you if it's gonna make you feel that way, Pop. Gee, I'll go anywheres with you if you only promise not to lose your head."

"Jest the sight uv that man'll make me lose my head, Skippy—I know it. But so long as yer make me promise—I won't give him the worst uv it, if I kin help it."

Skippy knew his father well enough to accept just that much and hope for the best. He went to the old battered trunk, took out a worn sweater and while still drawing it on followed Toby outside.

They descended the rope ladder in silence and got into the shabby boat. Toby turned over the motor and Skippy took his place at the bow to watch for drifting logs for the little kicker had not a light. Toby's former nocturnal occupations had made it necessary for him to dispense with this appurtenance and now, as he explained to his inquiring son, it had become a habit to roam the river without illumination, knowing as he did every square foot of it. Besides, he had come to love the solitude of darkness.

Skippy looked all about him, not exactly at his ease. The inlet was black and at times the starlit sky seemed so far away as to be but a mirage. Perhaps there wasn't a star in all the heavens, he would try to tell himself. All was black night and the muffled motor purred with a hushed monotony that affected him strangely. He fervently hoped that they would not be long in reaching the river where he could breathe without feeling that he was going to choke.

He knew he was afraid and he knew it really had nothing to do with the inlet or the black, silent night. It was a nameless dread that had seized him and, try as he would, he could not shake it off.

Instinctively, he felt that they shouldn't go on to Josiah Flint's yacht that night.

***

CHAPTER V

THE APOLLYON

Skippy felt better when the boat nosed out into the river. He raised his worried face to the clear salt breeze and let it blow over his hot cheeks. Lights blinked here and there on the dark water and a tug chortled by noisily. Then on the far shore he saw a cable light, and a ship ran clear of it before she dropped her mooring anchor.

Toby said nothing but sat in a lugubrious silence as he steered the little craft downstream. Skippy stared hard at the spray foaming against the bow; his mind was not on drifting logs. He turned to his father, scanned his face anxiously, then peered downstream again.

"Is Mr. Flint's yacht much further, Pop?" he asked after a few minutes.

"No, we oughta soon be on top uv her," came the hoarse reply. "Yer can't miss her—she's got her name sprawled fore an' aft in great big gold letters. It's some fancy name called A—Apollyon. That's it. Kindo highfalutin name, hey? Like all them there Flints."

"How many Flints are there, Pop?"

"Jest two now, like me an' you. Ol' Flint an' his son, Buck. His real name's Harry. Anyway folks call him Buck. But he's got it better'n you, Sonny. Much better. Besides he's old enough ter take his father's place in the dirty business, though I heerd not so long ago that Buck ain't uv a mind with the old man an' lets Marty Skinner help run the works. They say Buck's terrible honest an' all fer the law but Skinner's nothin' but a rat."

"Well, maybe Buck'll take over his father's business some day and make it pay without havin' smugglin' an' things like that, huh Pop?"

"Mebbe, but not if that crook Skinner keeps his ball in the game. Still, I heerd it said that Ol' Flint's business has always paid good enough without him doin' dirty work fer easy money. But that's what a miser he is—he's gotta have a crooked side line so's ter pile up his millions in a coupla years. He ain't willin' like the rest uv these shipowners 'round here ter wait an' let a honest fortune pile up, say, in twenty years or so. He can't be honest, Ol' Flint can't, not even with a poor man like me, an' Skinner's the same breed uv cats."

They were approaching a wide bend in the river. Anchored launches and trim sailboats dotted the shadowy water like immaculate sentinels. Skippy's restless eyes roved over the silent scene until he espied the graceful sweep of a yacht's bow projecting out of the shadows into the line of its anchor light. Simultaneously he saw great gold letters spelling out the name *Apollyon* and it occurred to him how modest and neat was the brass lettering of the *Minnie M. Baxter* in contrast.

The white, dainty craft swayed ever so gently on the slight swell and Skippy was lost in envy. He bethought himself of the sprawling uncouth barge and for a moment wondered why things were like this; why a man of Josiah Flint's sort could own this dainty, spotless yacht while his father who wanted so much to be honest had not even the worth of the hard-earned barge.

For the first time, he understood how bitter and revengeful his father must feel. He too felt bitter and revengeful as they got closer to the *Apollyon*. Something began to smolder in his boy's heart; something wholly alien to his cheerful, wholesome nature. But he was aware of nothing of this, save that he felt like sneering aloud at this proud, complacent craft swaying before his eyes. In a wild fancy he imagined her to be mocking his father and himself for daring to hope that Josiah Flint would make restitution.

A dim light shone amidships and save for the anchor lights the rest of the yacht was in darkness. Skippy stared hard at her and suddenly saw something skimming away from her port side.

He leaned far over the prow of the little motor boat until he saw that the object was a kicker like their own with its engine muffled. In whispered words he drew Toby's attention to it.

"Wonder where she's been and where she's goin' to, huh Pop?" he queried.

"That ain't none uv our business, Skippy," his father answered staring up at the *Apollyon*. "Folks on the river don't think uv them things this time uv night. They know a muffled engine's one that ain't carin' ter be heard, same as I got one fer mine."

"We could have ours taken off now, huh Pop? It ain't any more use now, is it?"

"That all depends, Sonny. It all depends on Ol' Flint," Toby said softly. "Now here we are an' the less said, the better."

"Ahoy!" called a voice in deep, soft tones from above. "Who's below?"

Father and son glanced up to see the head and shoulders of a burly man leaning over the glistening rail. Skippy saw Toby stiffen determinedly.

"Ol' Flint aboard?" he asked.

"Yeah," the man answered suppressing a yawn. "He's in his cabin amidships. Lookin' for him?"

"Yeah."

"Move the kicker aft an' come aboard. Old man was talkin' with Mr. Skinner when I come on duty two hours ago. His light's still on so he's readin' likely."

The little boat moved aft with hardly a splash and the next moment Toby was scrambling up the ladder. Skippy listened intently as his father set foot on the *Apollyon's* deck.

"Want me to tell him he's got a caller?" the man suddenly asked.

"Nope. Thanks jest the same," Toby was saying. "I even got half an idee that mebbe he expects me."

"Awright, buddy," said the man heartily. "You'll find him 'midships like I told you. There where the little light is."

Skippy heard the soft tread of his father's step along the deck. A door closed and after an interval of silence he looked up to see that the man was still there, bending over the rail and apparently staring at him.

"Your Dad, hey kid?" he asked, catching Skippy's upturned eyes.

"My Pop," Skippy corrected, chuckling. He liked the man's hearty voice. "You work aboard this yacht, Mister?"

"Second mate, that's what. Easy job summers when the old man's busy. All we do is to sleep and keep the old girl ship-shape."

"Old girl?"

"Yeah, this scow."

"Some scow!" Skippy laughed. "She's pretty swell, I'll say. Not much trouble keepin' *her* ship-shape, huh?"

"Naw. There ain't enough to keep us busy an' it makes a swab lazy. Same's me tonight. Here I am the only one on duty (there ain't no need for more'n one, anchored here like we are) and things are so quiet what do I do but fall sound asleep! I'd sat me down and I hear the old man bawlin' Mr. Skinner out fierce. Then I guess I was dozin' a spell 'fore I heard the sound of a muffled motor aft. Dreamed it, I guess, and I dreamed I heard somebody comin' out from the boss's quarters 'midships. Anyways, I finally woke up and when I come to the rail I see you folks. Guess that's what I was hearin' in my dreams all the time, hey?"

"Maybe," said Skippy. "Our motor's muffled, I guess you noticed already, but you might 'a' heard another kicker like ours too because one was aft when we came along."

"Guess maybe that's what it was then," said the second mate pleasantly. "Just somebody bein' a little cautious, like. Still I got to quit bein' so lazy nights and do my duty by *Polly* like the old man pays me for."

"*Polly?*"

The second mate laughed softly and Skippy fancied that his mischievous wink penetrated the darkness.

"*Apollyon—Polly* for short, kid! *Apollyon* is too highfalutin for able seamen, hey?"

"That's what I thought, Mister. I never heard it before. Gee whiz, what's it mean anyway?"

The second mate paused a moment.

"From what I could make out from the Cap'n it was the name of a Greek story or somethin'. You know—one of them real old Greeks thousands of years back. And this *Apollyon* was a evil spirit or somethin' like that, and folks called 'im the Destroyer! Ain't that a name for you?"

Skippy nodded and looked at the graceful ship with a new interest. Evil spirit? Destroyer? A queer name indeed for such a dainty craft. Why should Josiah Flint give that beautiful hull such an evil name? The sound of a dull thump interrupted his thoughts.

"I couldn't work on a ship with a name like that," he said to the second mate at length.

"Why?" the man laughed. "Superstitious?"

"I wouldn't say that," Skippy answered seriously. "At least I never thought I was sup-super-superstitious more'n most kids. But it don't seem exactly fair callin' a nice ship like that the destroyer or an evil spirit or whatever *Apollyon* really means. Gee, I've heard my Pop say that a ship kinda gets lookin' like its name an' actin' like its name after a while. That's why he named the barge he bought from Mr. Flint after my mother; the *Minnie M. Baxter* she's called. He said she'd be the nicest barge on the river if she took after my mother. But so far it ain't worked out," he added wistfully.

"No?" the second mate inquired sympathetically.

Skippy summed up the whole story of his father's misfortune in a few words. Particularly did he stress Toby's grief over Josiah Flint's wilful deception in the transaction.

"And so your Pop's come to make the old man come across, hey?

Well, I don't blame him." The man lowered his voice to a mere whisper. "I only hope he don't get the boss in a nasty temper 'cause he's not one to give in and he sounded like he was good and sore when he was bawlin' out Mr. Skinner. Besides, he ain't the one to admit he cheated your pop either. Still...."

A low moan startled them both and suddenly a door slammed, followed by the sound of someone running along the deck. Skippy stood straight up in the motor boat and listened intently.

He knew those footsteps and he knew what was in the mind that directed them with such force. His father never hurried, much less ran, unless he was terribly angered or pained or....

He dared not complete that thought, nor did he have need to, for his father's drawn, white face was already looking down at him from above the rail and Skippy read there all that he needed to know.

Something terrible had happened.

***

CHAPTER VI

A STRANGE STORY

The little motor boat had left the *Apollyon* far behind, ignoring shouts from its deck to halt, before Skippy dared break the tense silence.

"Gee, Pop," he stammered fearfully, "what happened between you and Mr. Flint anyway, huh? Because you didn't even say goodnight to the mate an' you got in the boat an' told me so cranky an' all to push off before I got a chance to say goodnight to him, either—gee whiz! I never seen you act so funny before in my life. What's the matter, huh?"

Toby Dare groaned and buried his face between his hands. Then, for what seemed to Skippy an interminable time, he rocked to and fro and the groans that escaped him were distressing to the waiting boy.

Finally Skippy could stand it no longer.

"Pop, you gotta tell me what's the matter! Gee, it's somethin' terrible the way...."

"Sonny," Toby interposed brokenly, "git back ter the *Minnie M. Baxter* jest as quick as yer kin! I got ter put as much water between me—me an'—an' *him* as it's possible ter put."

"Pop?"

"It's like a dream, Sonny—a bad dream—a terrible dream. I can't make head or tail uv it yet. I went ter his cabin 'midships like that mate told me...."

"Yes?" Skippy encouraged.

   Among the River Pirates

"I knocked on the door an' I could uv sworn I heard a kinda grunt like Ol' Flint does. He's a man uv few words. Anyways, I goes in an' there he's sittin' in a big chair with a funny grin on his face."

"Grinnin' at *you*, Pop?" Skippy asked clenching his straight white teeth.

"That's what I thought an' right away I got wild," Toby answered running his hands nervously through his disheveled hair. "I forgot what I promised—I forgot everythin' 'ceptin' the way he'd cheated me an' I got tellin' him so but he didn't say nothin', but jest kep' sittin' there a-grinnin' that funny way. Well, I knowed as how he always was a man uv few words but I thought he could stop grinnin' an' at least say *somethin'*. But he didn' an' that's what made me see red—I thought he was a-makin' fun uv me, sorta, an'——"

"You didn't go for him?" Skippy interposed fearfully.

"Sonny, I jest sorta lost my head," answered Toby brokenly. "I kin hardly remember what happened 'ceptin' I realized all uv a sudden that I had my hands 'round his throat an' I was chokin' him."

"And didn't he make any noise or anythin'?" Skippy was horrified.

"That's what made me let go. I got wise right then that somethin' was funny 'cause he didn't let a sound outa him all the time. His eyes seemed ter git funnier lookin' though, but he kep' on grinnin' jest the same. Then I let go quick an' *plop*—over he fell, head first he fell an' that's when I saw it——"

"*What?*"

"That he'd been shot in the back," Toby whispered looking about uneasily.

"*Pop!*"

"Sure as guns, Skippy," Toby moaned pitifully. "Then I knew he musta been dead all the time—even before I got in the room."

Skippy too groaned.

"How—how could he sit up like that then, if he really was *dead?*" he asked with an audible gulp.

"That's what I've been wonderin' an' all I kin think is that whoever did it, sat him up that way after it happened. I could see in his bedroom off uv the room he was sittin' in an' papers was lyin' all 'round like as if there'd been a scrap."

"With somebody else," Skippy murmured as if to himself. Then, in a frightened whisper: "What then, Pop?"

"All I could do was stand there like a crazy man," Toby groaned. "I don't even remember how long I stood there. It's all like part uv that nightmare so I can't remember."

"I know, Pop." Skippy tried to sound comforting. "Who—what groaned that time? The second mate and me heard it plain's anythin'."

"Me. That was when I knew he was dead! It jest sorta come ter me full in the face an' I was so full uv fright that I had ter let it out some way."

Skippy turned around and for a few moments searched the face of his unhappy father.

"Pop—Pop," he faltered, "just one thing I can't understand—why—why didn't you tell the second mate, an' me, right then? Why—why didn't you spurt it right out an' not run away when you know you didn't do it?"

"Who'd believe it?" Toby answered hopelessly. "There was the mark uv my fingers on his throat—*there they was!* I'd even have ter admit ter that mate that I was mad enough ter choke Ol' Flint ter death—he could see my fingers there ter prove it, couldn't he? Well, why wouldn't he think I give him an automatic in the back afterwards, hey? Why wouldn't he?"

"*But, Pop!* If you only had said *sumpin!*"

"I wanted ter git away from that awful grinnin' face. As far away as I c'd get. I—I couldn't stay there ter tell nobody *nothin'*, Skippy. Besides, do I know I didn't choke him ter—ter..." He sobbed a moment, then looked up. "Mebbe 'twasn't the automatic what really got him, Skippy—mebbe 'twas *me*, hey?"

Skippy reached out and grasped Toby's damp flannel shirt sleeve in agony.

"Pop, it wasn't you—I know it—*I just feel it!*" he cried. "I can tell from all you told me about him grinnin' like from the time you got inside the room." He hesitated a moment, then: "You don't remember him makin' a sound at all?" he asked, anxiously peering into his father's face.

"Not one sol'tary sound, Sonny—I didn't hear a one!"

Skippy sighed and again took up the task of steering the little motor boat upstream. His tired young face, however, had taken on a new look of resolution.

"You're tired, Pop, an' I'm gonna take you back to the *Minnie M. Baxter.* Then I'm gonna turn this kicker straight back and head her downstream again an' I'm goin' aboard that *Apollyon* an' explain the whole thing. I'll tell 'em everythin' like you told me an' I bet they'll believe it all right 'cause they'll see that my Pop couldn't kill anybody."

Toby said nothing but continued to rock back and forth with his head in his hands.

"Maybe—maybe you're not so tired an' you'd turn 'round with me an' go back an' tell 'em, huh Pop?" Skippy returned anxiously.

"Skippy," Toby cried hoarsely, "jest now I wanta go back ter the *Minnie M. Baxter* an' think. Like a good boy don't talk about it no more till we get there, hey?"

Skippy, bewildered, promised that he wouldn't, and let the little kicker out to the best of her ability. From time to time he heard the miserable sighs of his father, and over and over again he told himself the story of Josiah Flint's strange death just as Toby had told it. But with each recurring thought, a strange suspicion asserted itself and clamored so hard in the boy's conscious mind that he was forced to recognize that it was a doubt, a small one, but nevertheless a doubt of his father's story.

And by the time they were once more on board the *Minnie M. Baxter,* Skippy was fearful that possibly, after all, his father might be the actual murderer of Josiah Flint!

***

CHAPTER VII

FOR SKIPPY

Skippy washed the dishes and cleaned up the cabin, then made some fresh coffee. He put the two cups on a little tin tray and carried it out on deck where his father sat disconsolately puffing a pipe.

"I made this good an' careful, Pop," he said, handing Toby a cup of the steaming beverage. "Maybe it'll make you feel better, it's so hot."

Toby took the proffered cup and smiled wanly.

"Yer think your Pop's a coward, takin' on this way?" he asked anxiously.

Skippy flushed and, to cover his embarrassment, sat down on a stool a little distance away.

"Nah, I don't think that, Pop," he said at length. "I guess I know how kinda crazy an' different you'd act after seem' that. Gee, it musta been pretty awful to make you act so different."

"I know how yer mean by different, Sonny, but I ain't blamin' yer. I know it must look funny, but it ain't. Besides I ain't a coward 'bout it. If I'd told the mate right on the spot, he'd had ter keep me till the police come. Then what would happened ter *you*? Even if I give myself up now they'll hold me on charges an' the law's that slow, it'll be months mebbe 'fore I kin clear myself."

"But that'd be better'n lettin' 'em think you was the one that killed Mr. Flint, wouldn't it?"

"I thought mebbe we could run somewheres out west or the like, hey Skippy? Yer don't know what the law is once yer git in its fist. If

     Among the River Pirates

they can't find nobody else they'll pin it on me no matter what we say—I know it! So we might's well take our duds an' beat it now."

"Pop, you're not talkin' like yourself. You got sorta crazy on accounta thinkin' how all this'll hurt me. Gee whiz, forget about me, because you can't have the cops thinkin' you did it, when you didn't! Gee, I'll get along somehow, honest I will, Pop. I'll get along better to know you did what was right an' told the truth. An' even the law I bet can see when a man's tellin' the truth an' they'll let you out quick—so will you go for my sake, Pop?"

Toby brought a hairy fist down on his bony knees.

"It's fer yer sake that I didn't want ter go near 'em, Skippy," he said vehemently. "But if yer promise yer Pop ter stay good an' all till they let me out, I don't care. Fer my sake I *wanta* go!"

"Gee, Pop, I'm glad!"

Toby drank his coffee with a determined gulp, then got up and stalked into the cabin with the empty cup. When he came out, he held out his hands to Skippy.

"C'mon, then, Sonny," he said gripping the boy by the shoulders, "we'll be a-gittin' back ter the *Apollyon* 'fore too much water slips inter the bay, hey?"

"Just what I was thinkin' of, Pop," Skippy answered and averted his head so that his father should not see the tears swimming in his eyes. "And, Pop, you're kinda calm now, ain't you? Calm enough to remember better'n when we were comin' down?"

Toby Dare nodded wearily.

"What yer wanta know, Skippy?"

"Just that you're good an' sure that you didn't hear him make a noise from the time you first seen him till you ran outa the room?"

"Sure, I'm sure, Sonny. And like I told you, the grin was the same too."

"Then he *was* dead, Pop—dead all the time, an' somebody with an automatic did it because the second mate said he dreamed he heard somebody runnin' an' then he heard a muffled kicker shoving off aft like I saw when we come along. Whoever had that automatic was in that kicker, Pop. I got a hunch about it."

"I hope the coppers believe you, Sonny. But c'mon, we'll take the chance. Anyways, I'll tell what I know."

They walked forward together and were just about to descend when they saw a long, dark painted launch shoot alongside of the *Minnie M. Baxter*. As Skippy and his father leaned over to get a better view they were blinded with the glaring rays of a searchlight.

"*Coppers, Pop!*" Skippy hissed. "It's the coppers!"

"COPPERS, POP!" SKIPPY HISSED. "IT'S THE COPPERS!"
Frontispiece

Toby gripped his son's trembling fingers in his own.

"Don't move, Dare!" a deep voice commanded from the police launch.

"I'm not," Toby answered hoarsely.

"We'll be right up. Stay right where you are."

"Pop an' I were just comin'," Skippy cried to them, "that is, we were just goin' back to the yacht—the *A—Apollyon* an' tell them how it all really happened. Pop ran away on accounta me, but after we talked about it he decided to go back an' tell.... Mr. Flint was dead before Pop got there—*he was; honest!*"

"Oh yeah?" laughed the first officer to reach the deck. "Now that's interestin'. But I'd wait till the rest of the gang gets up, kid, because they all got ears too."

Skippy watched them troop up until the last man set foot on the barge's worn deck. Six men, he thought, with not a little fear. How weak would his father's story seem to these frowning cops? Would they believe him as he had believed him?

His fingers were entwined in his father's in a tight grip and yet he had the feeling that Toby was already snatched away from him. Now that the police confronted them he was terribly afraid and in that instant his hopes fled as quickly as the stars in the face of gathering storm clouds overhead.

Then Toby spoke in his hoarse, broken voice....

***

CHAPTER VIII

ALONE

Skippy's hopes were somewhat rekindled during Toby's recital of his visit to the yacht. The story sounded so straightforward as he told it, that it did not seem possible that these representatives of the law could find a single flaw in it. And yet to his utter dismay they found more than a flaw in it; they found it sufficiently damning to threaten his unhappy father with certain conviction.

They had already seen Inspector Jones and had had his word for it that Toby Dare had threatened to "fix Josiah Flint," and there was also the corroboration of the inspector's men. There was also the strongly incriminating statement of the second mate of the *Apollyon* and the charge that Toby refused to stop when called to from the yacht by Skinner.

"My Pop never carried a gun!" Skippy cried in protest. "You can't say that he did!"

"There's a robbery charge too," said one of the officers sternly. "You went to Flint's yacht because you were sore and Inspector Jones heard you crack that it would be bad for Flint if he didn't kick in for the loss of the barge. It adds up swell for a jury."

"Yeah," said another, "and when Flint give you the razz like you're trying to tell us, you burn up, shoot him, then you choke him and frisk him to get that three hundred with plenty interest back. Your fingerprints on his throat are the only fingerprints we found. What did you do with the gun—throw it in the river?"

Among the River Pirates

Toby denied it all with a groan, and Skippy sidled up to his father and held on to his arm with a gesture of protection. The officers frowned for there is neither time nor place for sentiment in the progress of the law. They had come to arrest Toby Dare for the murder and robbery of Josiah Flint and all Skippy's pleading would not thwart them.

The faint boom of thunder sounded as Toby was led into the police launch and a flash of lightning streaked the black sky just above the *Minnie M. Baxter*. But Skippy was indifferent to everything save the hopeless, staring look that his father gave him as their eyes met.

He fought back the tears bravely and smiled his bravest.

"Now, Pop, stop thinking about me again, huh!" he cried desperately. "Gee whiz, I'll be swell—I promise I will so will you cheer up an' everythin', huh? Because you gotta prove you're tellin' the truth an' never had a gun so how could you do what they say you did? So will you cheer up if I tell you I'll be all right, no matter what?"

Toby Dare's troubled face lighted with a smile.

"Skippy, boy," he gulped, "I kin do anythin' when I hear yer talk like that. Jest hearin' yer say yer'll be a good boy's enough fer me."

"All right, then, Pop," Skippy said, forcing a laugh. "So we won't even say so long 'cause they'll let you come back in a day or so, I bet."

"Sure," Toby assured him. "They're bound ter let me."

And that was all, for the launch chugged off leaving Skippy strangely numb and bewildered. He watched the snakelike movements of the trim craft as she darted through the inlet but soon the darkness enfolded her from view. After a few moments they switched on their running lights but there was too much distance between them for the boy to see his father and so he turned his back to the inlet and slowly walked toward the little cabin.

Not a light had appeared the length or breadth of the whole barge colony since the police launch slipped up to the *Minnie M. Baxter* yet Skippy knew that every man and woman in Brown's Basin was awake and watching all that had transpired. His father had told him that these strange, lawless people had a surprising faculty for learning of the law's arrival in the inlet. And hating the law as they did, they kept silently out of its sight, nor did they want to be drawn into it through another's troubles.

Notwithstanding this knowledge, Skippy had the feeling that he had only to call out and ask for help for himself and his father, and his lawless neighbors would immediately respond. Yet that is just what Toby had warned him against. Moreover, his promise to avoid dubious company was not ten minutes old.

And so he resolved to bear his troubles manfully and alone, though never in his life had he so wanted the warmth and sympathy of human companionship. He was young enough to be afraid, yet old enough to feel ashamed of it. But the events of the day and his father's unhappy plight finally proved too much for him and with trembling under lip he sought the shelter of the cabin.

A few minutes later a terrific storm broke over the river and swept through the Basin relentlessly. Rain lashed against the tiny windows of the cabin on the *Minnie M. Baxter* and the wind moaned eerily in and out of the inlet.

Skippy buried his tousled head under a pillow in his bunk and tried to stifle the sobs that would not stop. His heart raced madly in his breast every time he thought of his father and his fears increased with every crash of thunder. Could it possibly be that his father wouldn't come back?

He squirmed farther under the bedclothes. He would have shut out his thoughts if that had been possible. Presently he heard a muffled knocking at the cabin door.

***

CHAPTER IX

A VISITOR

Skippy sat up instantly, threw off the bedclothes and slid to the floor. Then he hurried to the little table and lighted the lamp, meanwhile glancing toward the door uneasily. The knock sounded again; this time insistently.

He rushed to the door and swung it open. A man stood before him in the pelting rain, the tallest, broadest man he had ever seen in his life. He could not have been out of his twenties and had a large, rather amiable looking face; so large, indeed, that it made his blue eyes seem small and insignificant.

A MAN STOOD BEFORE HIM IN THE PELTING RAIN.

As Skippy waited questioningly, he moved his ponderous neck above his upturned coat collar and smiled, a slow, secretive smile. Then he half turned and glanced quickly toward the inlet, before he spoke.

"Sure and be ye Toby's kid?" he asked with a slight brogue. "Can I come in? And where's Toby bein' at this hour?" He walked into the cabin quickly.

The ghost of a smile flitted across Skippy's tear-stained cheeks as he closed the door.

"Sure, sure, come in!" he said hospitably. "Pop ain't here. He's...."

"'Tis all right, so 'tis," the stranger interposed pleasantly, and calmly divested himself of his wet clothing. "I got nothin' but time. Your ould man told me I'd always be welcome in his diggins so here I be. 'Tis too bad 'bout this scow, though. I only got wise tonight that the inspectors told Toby the *Minnie M. Baxter* was junk. Bad cess to 'em. So Flint gypped Toby on it, did he?"

"An' how!" Skippy answered dismally. "Gee, gee...."

The man got up and waving his hands deprecatingly, made a quick movement toward one of the windows on the inlet side. He bent his huge frame in a stooping posture and after rubbing the steam from the diminutive pane, he peered out intently.

Suddenly he turned back and smiled his slow, secretive smile.

"I ain't exactly aisy in me mind, kid," he explained with a low chuckle. "I be keepin' a weather eye on thim coppers. They're curious like 'bout some stuff and I ain't in the spirit to answer thim. They got me barge and that's enough, so 'tis."

"You ain't Big Joe Tully?" Skippy asked.

"That be callin' the turn, kid. S'pose your Pop give ye an earful 'bout me. Well, I started out shootin' straight like he did, but whilst Flint's got the monop'ly on shippin' and the like on this river, a guy's a million to one, so he is."

"Mr. Flint won't have it no more," Skippy gulped. "I guess you ain't heard...."

"*What?*" asked Big Joe Tully reaching in his pocket for a cigarette.

"He's dead—he was killed tonight." Tears rushed to Skippy's eyes again. "An' my Pop's been sorta accused, Mr. Tully," he added, and blurted out the whole story.

Tully was puffing energetically on his cigarette when Skippy finished.

"Now don't ye be worryin' kid," he said sympathetically. "If that ol' rat was dead when Toby got there they can't do nothin' to him. Toby'll be home tomorrow, so he will, I bet."

Skippy felt instantly cheered. He was beginning to feel glad of Big Joe's comforting presence when he bethought himself of the man's dubious activities on the river. Wasn't it this man and his ilk that his father had warned him against? Men who weren't honest? The boy sat down on his bunk to think it over.

     Among the River Pirates

To his surprise, Tully had got up and was putting on his coat and hat. Immediately, Skippy forgot that he was considering the moral aspect of an invitation to the man to stay; he forgot all his father's warnings against association with the river gentry, and thought only of the void that Tully's sudden departure would make in the long night.

"I thought you said you were gonna stay, Mr. Tully?" he said with evident disappointment. "Gee, now you ain't, huh?"

"'Tis sorry I be, kid," said Big Joe with a friendly wink. "I did think along thim lines when I come in, but since the coppers been nosin' 'round here tonight, I'll be mosyin' along. They might come back and spot me here so I'd better be takin' the air."

"Did they catch you carryin' *stuff?*" Skippy asked, interested. "Is that why?"

"Sure and they did that. Somewan tipped off the police—somewan what was jealous I wasn't carryin' *their* stuff." He laughed lightly. "The coppers hook ye either way, so they do. Look how quick they come after Toby and they knew he was on the up and up! So I says, does it pay?" Then, seeing the shadow on Skippy's face, he added: "But sure you'll be seein' Toby back tomorrow, kid. They can't be keepin' him when he didn't do it."

"He didn't do it, so they can't!" Skippy echoed.

"'Tis a cinch, so 'tis," said Big Joe Tully with an awkward attempt to sympathize. "Be hittin' the hay now, kid, an' ye'll be seein' Toby tomorrow or me name ain't Joe Tully. Now I'll be swingin' into me kicker and chug her up the river till daylight. I'll be layin' low a while and some day I'll be seein' ye and Toby. Be watchin' the old step. S'long."

He went out like a breeze and Skippy soon heard the chug of his engine. Another craft muffled so that the ears of the law would not hear its approach! The boy made a mental grimace at the thought of all this muffled life on the river, Big Joe Tully included. His inherent love of clean living and honesty had come to the fore as his father had wanted it to. And honesty and clean living *did* pay despite what Tully had said. Certainly it would pay his father tomorrow! He lay back on his bunk and closed his burning eyes.

Tomorrow was almost here ... almost....

***

CHAPTER X

A SUGGESTION

Many tomorrows had come and gone before Skippy saw his father again and then it was under circumstances that the lonely boy had not contemplated. The shadow of prison walls already threatened Toby Dare for the rest of his natural life; conviction was certain.

Skippy returned to the *Minnie M. Baxter* toward noon. It threatened to be a sultry day; the air was heavy and still, and a sickening blue haze hung over the inlet. Brown's Basin, always more or less apathetic under the glare of noonday, was unusually silent and Skippy listened in vain for the cheering sound of a human voice.

He set about preparing lunch, but it was a half-hearted, pathetic attempt, for the Dare larder was getting dangerously bare. He had been living on an almost exclusive diet of pancakes for more than a week past and Nature was beginning to retaliate for Skippy was far from being a robust boy.

He pushed back his plate after a time, hurried out of the cabin and got into his motor boat. It was his only consolation during the interminable days and nights of his father's continued absence and on this particular day his heart warmed toward it with a new, affectionate thought.

His fishing tackle was assembled at his feet and he set the nose of the little boat downstream as soon as he reached the river. Fog horns pierced the still, hazy air with their dismal warnings and the screams of steam winches and tooting whistles echoed and reechoed about the boy's tousled head.

He watched the passing river traffic abstractedly, particularly the lumbering and heavily-laden barges moving along in the wake of chortling tugs. The sight of them always made him think of his father and of what might have been, and the more he saw of them the more did the feeling grow within him that it was a strange and unjust law that could take his father away from him. Moreover, he could not understand why a jury would not believe his father's straightforward story, which proved so clearly to him that another hand had taken Josiah Flint's life.

Hadn't the police found that the rich man had been robbed of a considerable sum of money and hadn't they admitted that it was neither on Toby's person nor on the barge? Skippy remembered only too well the day when the police ransacked the *Minnie M. Baxter* fore and aft for Josiah Flint's money. But their search was futile, as he knew it would be, and although they now had ample proof that poverty threatened him, they still insisted that the stolen money had been hidden by his unhappy father.

But Skippy did not consider the testimony of Marty Skinner that he, on returning to his employer's stateroom, saw Toby Dare with his arm out the porthole (from which a clever and venomous prosecuting attorney drew the inference for the jury that Toby was disposing of the pistol from which the fatal shot was fired). Skinner did not swear he saw any weapon, but his testimony, linked with the other evidence, made for a strong circumstantial case.

Skinner also testified that he had rushed to his employer's side as Toby raced from the room; that upon discovering that Josiah Flint had been shot he chased after the squatter and shouted to him, as he made off in his kicker, to no avail. The second mate corroborated the testimony that Toby failed to heed the cries for him to halt.

While the pistol had not been found, Inspector Jones and his men testified that Toby had threatened to fix Josiah Flint because he felt he had been cheated of his life savings of $300 in buying a rotten barge from Flint. That, the prosecutor insisted to the jury, furnished the motive for the crime. Altogether he made a case which convinced the twelve men, but it did not convince Skippy for he could not be convinced that his father was guilty.

Skippy was deep in his bitter reflections and did not see the familiar launch of the harbor inspectors until it was almost upon him. Inspector Jones' bright and smiling face came alongside of him with startling suddenness.

"Well, Skippy!" he said pleasantly. "How's the boy?"

Skippy winced and a frown darkened his face. He could not forget that Inspector Jones' testimony had helped to take his father from him.

"I feel sick on accounta my Pop, that's what," said he bitterly. "You helped make things worse for him too, Mr. Jones, on account of the things you told about what he said that day after you inspected the *Minnie M. Baxter*."

Inspector Jones' bland countenance looked immediately troubled.

"I told the truth, Skippy," he said kindly. "I told only what your father had said and my men were there to prove it."

"You needn't have said that Pop said he was gonna *fix* Mr. Flint 'cause you mighta known he really didn't mean it. Pop was mad then, but he promised me before we left for the *Apollyon* that night that he wouldn't lose his head. Gee, he's even sworn since he didn't take Mr. Flint's life an' don't you suppose I know when my Pop's tellin' the truth?"

"I guess so," Inspector Jones answered with real feeling in his voice; "I guess you know your Pop better than anybody, Skippy. I'm sorry, the law required me to testify against him. But it was my duty—can't you see?"

"Then you believe they'll be keepin' my Pop in jail when he's innocent, too, huh?" Skippy asked excitedly.

"I'm rather inclined to believe that your father didn't shoot Flint," answered the inspector. "But I can't do anything about it, Skippy, and I doubt if my testimony alone would convict him. It's that District-Attorney and Marty Skinner that's made it so tough for your father.

You know Skinner swore he saw Toby at the porthole and the D. A. put it over to the jury that he was dropping the gun which did the job."

"Yeah, but that diver didn't find no gun," Skippy replied, "an' my Pop swore he wasn't near no porthole an' besides nobody tried findin' out about that kicker that was around when we come up. I'll betcha the feller what did the killin' got away in it."

"You're right about not finding the gun, Skippy," Inspector Jones nodded thoughtfully. "I'll look into the kicker angle some more."

"Say, thanks, Mr. Jones, me'n Pop we'd be so thankful, we would. Maybe if I went to see Mr. Skinner he'd help us 'cause I guess hard as he is he'll see I don't tell lies even to get my Pop free. Maybe I oughta go right away to see him, huh?"

Inspector Jones nodded thinking how futile the boy's errand would be. But he had boys of his own and he did not want to jolt the lad out of his pleasant dream. So all he said was: "The sooner the better, because I hear he's going on the *Apollyon* for a week's cruise. You know Buck Flint has gone to Europe and now Skinner, who was only Josiah Flint's yes-man for years, is ruling the roost and living high on a millionaire's yacht. Buck says he won't ever board her so it's pretty soft for Skinner. He's got the boat anchored just outside in the bay, ready to nose her out to sea after nightfall. If you get right on down there, you'll catch him aboard, sure."

Skippy smiled his thanks and turned his little motor over. The inspector waved his hand.

"From the sound of that kicker," he shouted, "I take it you've lost Toby's muffler?"

"Sure," Skippy answered laughing, "what do I need with a muffler, huh? 'Cepting it might be better for fishin' with. But gee, I should worry about livin' on fish if I can see Mr. Skinner, huh? Pop ought to be out by—by...."

"Tomorrow, eh?" Inspector Jones interposed turning his head aside and blowing his nose hard.

Among the River Pirates

"Nope," Skippy answered wistfully, "I won't say tomorrow 'cause then—oh well, it's too quick. But anyway, if I see Mr. Skinner it won't be long after tomorrow, I bet."

He had yet to learn from his bitter experience that tomorrow never comes.

***

CHAPTER XI

ALL OF A KIND

Skippy's little boat chugged out of the bay and around toward the Hook. It was late afternoon and the haze had deepened into an ominous sultriness. White caps danced atop the waves and off on the horizon black clouds and black sea met in dismal union. A flock of gulls swarmed about, flapping their huge wings between sky and sea with monotonous precision.

A miscellaneous collection of craft was anchored just outside the bay; sailboats, fishing smacks, dories and yachts of every size, and not the least of these was the shining hull of the lovely *Apollyon*. Skippy caught sight of her immediately and slowed his own little boat that he might have a better view of her in the light of day.

Her superstructure was painted a most delicate shade of green and Skippy understood then why he had imagined her to be of that ghostly whiteness below her anchor lights which shone like stars against that dark, memorable night. Too, the large gilt letters spelling out her queer name seemed not so ornate now as when he had first seen them.

His first reaction to the lovely yacht had been one of envy and admiration; it was so now and he tried hard not to think of the unhappy sequel that his first visit to the *Apollyon* had brought. Yet somehow he could not shake off the fear-inspiring memory of what the name really meant and he wondered if anything but evil could tread those spotless decks.

He chuckled a little and turned his motor boat toward the yacht. There were signs of a near-departure aboard and he caught sight of the

                                    Among the River Pirates

second mate resplendent in his spotless uniform and cap. Leaning over the forward rail, he recognized Skippy at once, and waved his hand.

"If it ain't the kid!" he called cheerfully. "Young Dare, hey? Well, you've come a ways."

"Sure," Skippy smiled. "I come down to see Mr. Skinner. It's awful particular what I gotta see him about."

"You look's if it might be a case of life or death at that," the second mate mused.

"It is a case of life, Mister—my Pop's whole life," said Skippy anxiously. "That's why I wanta see Mr. Skinner."

The second mate was all contrition. "Kid, I clean forgot about your Pop, 'deed I did. C'mon aboard. Sure Mr. Skinner'll be seein' you. 'Course I ain't promisin' you'll find him easy talkin' to 'cause he ain't. He's right set in his notions 'bout you Basin and river folks; he thinks you're all rascals."

"But his boss, ol' Flint——" Skippy began protesting.

"He knowed like you'n me and plenty others that the old boss was a tough egg—and between you'n me Skinner ain't no angel hisself—but that don't change his mind none."

Skippy realized this full well a little later when Marty Skinner refused to hear him, ordered him off the boat, and shouted that his father was a rogue and so was he.

Skippy rushed blindly out of the cabin. The door slammed behind him, the same door that had slammed behind his father on that tragic night. He had accomplished just nothing at all in that cabin of past horrors, nothing except to hear from a gentleman's lips what his kind really thought of river people.

And he, Skippy Dare, was one of the river people—himself, the son of a rogue!

***

CHAPTER XII

DRIFTING

Skippy nosed the motor boat toward the Hook. He had no thought of anything save that he was angry and hurt and wanted to feel the fresh, salt breeze blow over his burning face. He felt that he must think over this new and humiliating status in which Marty Skinner had so cruelly placed him, and he wanted to think of it where no one could see the unhappiness that it caused him.

He hadn't the heart to turn back toward the Basin and home. Home! He frowned at the word, for it seemed that the *Minnie M. Baxter* and all that it represented could bring him nothing now but recurring thoughts of the hated Skinner. All that the man had said had left its mark on the sensitive boy's mind and for the first time in his life he felt a bitter hatred toward a fellow being.

That Marty Skinner, old Josiah Flint's right-hand man, should call his father a rogue, was hardly to be endured. But if it were so, he reasoned in a calmer moment, then all the more reason for the blame to fall on the dead Josiah. Hadn't Old Flint himself been the worst rogue of all?

He was tempted to return and shout these thoughts so that all aboard the *Apollyon* might hear. He wanted to tell them what Toby had said about Josiah Flint making the despised Brown's Basin possible because of his selfish, unscrupulous dealings.

But, boy-like, Skippy's anger was soon reduced to a smoldering memory and his father's imminent incarceration was a thing that had to be faced. Just now he was forced to think of his own present situation, for a significant sputtering from the motor gave warning that he was about to have trouble.

He had not his father's knack for adjusting the rebellious motor, and so he decided to turn the boat about and make for the quieter waters of the bay. But just then the motor stalled and despite his earnest efforts, it refused to respond.

Skippy looked about him anxiously and saw that he had already been carried an alarming distance. Dusk was rapidly settling, hastened by the deepening haze and in a few moments the tide and undertow had swept him out of sight of all the anchored craft clustered about the *Apollyon*.

He looked hopefully toward the Hook but saw that it was useless to try and reach it even with the one oar that the little boat had in reserve. The tide was against him.

After a quick glance about, he hunted around among some neglected tools lying at his feet and picked out the searchlight. But that, too, refused to respond; the battery was dead. Then he looked for some matches only to meet with disheartening disappointment.

He got to his knees after that and worked furiously at the cold motor, squinting at his hopeless task in the near-darkness. The boom of thunder could be heard from out at sea, and with the swiftly passing minutes the storm came nearer and nearer until it broke directly overhead.

Lightning flashed across the drifting boat and Skippy dodged under the bow. There was something terrifying about the elements when one was alone and drifting steadily toward the sea in an open boat.

After a momentary lull, he crept out, not a little ashamed of his cowardice. He looked about, trying hard not to look or feel panicky despite the fact that he could see nothing of the Hook or anything else. Darkness and high, shadowy waves upon which the little boat bobbed were all that met his frightened gaze. Then a damp, cold wind began to blow.

He crouched down in the bottom of the boat with a feeling of dull despair. Rain pattered into an old rusty bait can that lay at his feet and he edged his shivering body closer under the bow. Curiously enough, he was quite calm now and the thought that his situation was dangerous did not enter his mind.

Skippy-like, he was thinking only that he was terribly hungry and more than anything else he wanted to eat.

***

CHAPTER XIII

LIGHTS

The thunder and lightning died away after a time but the rain continued. The constant boom of the sea gradually wore away some of Skippy's calm and he raised his head from time to time to gaze apprehensively at the dark sea rising all about him in mountainous waves.

The sky seemed a black void and at times as the little boat tossed about in the waves, he had the breath-taking sensation that he had turned turtle. Once, he mused about what probability there was of his being carried clear across the sea to some European port. He had heard of men being able to live without food or water from ten to fourteen days. Well, he had his fishing outfit, he reasoned hopefully; he needn't starve, but how to get water puzzled him.

After a few more minutes of tossing wildly about, he decided that the little boat could probably never stand an ocean voyage. With each succeeding wave it came perilously near to upsetting and he doubted that the craft could triumph over the angry sea much longer.

That contingency awoke a strong determination in him, for he got to his feet, reached for the oar and struggled valiantly to balance the boat against the oncoming foe. The rain soaked him through to the skin but he was not cold for he was kept in constant action trying to make one oar do the work of two.

He had lost all sense of time and direction; he thought only of keeping the boat balanced. That he could not keep it up very long did not occur to him, for he already felt the effects of the past week's malnutrition and his long journey from the Basin had fatigued him.

After what seemed an interminable time he caught a glimpse of a light, a faint gleam, but nevertheless a light. He gasped with joy and looked hard into the darkness to get a definite idea of its location. In point of fact he looked so hard he all but swamped the boat.

Great beads of perspiration stood out on his forehead when he righted the boat, but he came up triumphant on the crest of a wave. The exertion was too much for him, however; he felt inexpressibly weak and tired. His muscles ached and a giddiness in his head made him feel as if he must lie down.

But there was the light just ahead and he bent his frail body in a supreme effort to reach it. He was cheered because it did not seem to move and he ventured to hope that it might be on the shore. The main thing—it was a light, and light might reasonably be expected to mean rescue by all the rules of the game.

Suddenly a great arc of faint yellow light swept from behind and circled his head. He had come to no decision about its origin before it came again, a little brighter than before. Then after some minutes had passed and it had grown still brighter, it occurred to him that it was from the lighthouse at the Hook and the great light had gradually penetrated the fast dissolving haze.

He took heart at this because he knew he could not be so very far away from land. But he knew it was futile to even hope to get back there in his boat. It might be ten miles and it might be twenty. The great light at the Hook boasted a range of thirty miles on a clear night, he had heard his father say.

The light that gave him real hope was the heartening glimmer just ahead. He knew that it was not just because he wished it so fervently, but he could plainly see that it became brighter as the boat advanced.

Then suddenly he heard the faint ringing of a bell, which echoed eerily on the shifting wind.

***

CHAPTER XIV

THE BELL BUOY

He listened intently and thought that it came from the direction of the light. It rang again and again, each time a little louder. Suddenly, however, he was aware that the light seemed no longer stationary. He had the disheartening experience of realizing that his beacon of hope was a running light on a fishing smack. He felt like crying as he watched the shadowy hull gaining speed for he realized that she must have just started ahead, having waited for the wind to change.

Every wave carried her farther and farther away from the watching boy. If he had only got there just a little sooner, he thought dismally. But he had done the best he could. There was nothing left now but to sit and watch her swallowed up by the darkness and the mountainous seas and that had happened in a few minutes' time.

He was glad he had not been foolish enough to hope that he could reach her and overtake her, only to be disappointed and use up what little strength he had left. That at least was some satisfaction and it helped him bear his desperate plight a little more patiently.

The constant booming of the sea had a queer effect on his sensitive ears. He imagined himself to be hearing all sorts of noises, particularly the ringing of the bell. At times he could have sworn he heard it right at hand and at other times it seemed but a mocking echo.

The air was quite clear now, though the rain continued, and Skippy saw to his dismay that the boat was getting a little too full of water for his safety. He put down the oar for a while and bailed her out with his rusty bait can.

The little boat tossed against each rising wave like a feather; but he worked feverishly and trusted to luck that it would not upset. Then after a few minutes he was startled by the sound of the bell ringing right over his head. Before he had time to look up he felt the boat bump hard against something.

He was on his feet in a second and saw to his great surprise that the boat was alongside of a bell buoy.

It has been truly said that time and tide wait for no man and certainly Skippy was aware of this instantly, for in the next second a giant wave had washed him out of reach of the buoy. This realization made him desperate and he got into action to get back to it, for he well knew now that to drift on through the night would mean certain death.

With a swift movement he pushed his wet hair back from his high forehead. Then he bent over, got the oar and grabbed a rope, holding it tightly in his hand. And for fully five minutes he battled and struggled against the undertow.

His eyes were wide and staring from the strain and little streams of water ran down either cheek. His clothes from head to foot were weighted against him with water but he never stopped until he had brought the boat back against the buoy and in a second he had thrown the painter around it and pulled it taut.

That done he sank down in the bottom of the boat, exhausted.

For some time his mind was an utter blank. He was too tired and weak to think or even to care. But the rain beating steadily down on his unprotected body soon chilled him back into action and he got up and exercised his arms and legs.

As the buoy swayed upon each succeeding swell, the bell tolled mournfully. Its eerie echoes were faint and quickly lost in the noise of the pounding sea, and Skippy decided that no mariner ten minutes' sail from the bell was likely to look that way. Also, the quick wash of the sea prevented the bell from tolling its loudest and longest. Nothing but his own two hands could do that.

And so he did it.

For the next hour he bent his frail body over the swaying buoy and swung the cold, wet bell back and forth, back and forth. Peal after peal tolled forth dismally and though his eyes became blurred with weariness he knew that he had missed nothing, for nothing had passed for him to miss.

So it went on through the long, dark hours. He would take an interval of rest and then jump up to his vigil at the bell for fear he would fall asleep and miss some passing ship.

The night seemed interminable. Indeed, he began to believe that he had fallen asleep and that a day had passed and another night had come without his being aware of it, for never had he thought the dark hours were so long.

Morning came at last and with the first streak of light on the eastern horizon, hope came back anew. The rain gradually ceased and during Skippy's intervals of rest he watched, with not a little awe, the wonder of dawn at sea. Little by little the night fled before the roseate morn and soon the entire sky was flooded with soft light. And as the sun crept up out of the sea he stretched himself across the wet seats and relaxed.

Two hours later, he woke with the sun shining full in his face. He sat up, startled, and realized that his head was aching and that he felt stiff and chilled. Moreover, he felt sick with despair to think that he had slept away the hours of daylight, hours when a ship might have passed near enough for him to signal.

He stood up and scanned the sunlit water in all directions but there was not a sign of a sail, not a sign of a ship. In the distance, a gull soared high above the water and after a moment another one seemed to leap out of space and join it.

The tide was going out and the whole surface of the blue-green water seemed to roll on toward the horizon in a series of undulating hills. A gentle murmur filled the warm, sunlit air and Skippy could not believe that the booming surf of the past night had been anything but a bad dream.

He rang the bell for a time but had to give it up because of a terrible giddiness in his head. And so for hours, he sat anxiously scanning the illimitable sea and sky, hoping, hoping, hoping....

Noon came and passed and the sun scorched him cruelly. The boat, too, had become a constant source of anxiety for she developed a leak and had to be continually bailed out, and he was thankful that he had not obeyed a former impulse and tried to row her east in the hope that he would strike the Hook.

Toward mid-afternoon he was conscious of pains in his chest, and his hunger and thirst were becoming unbearable, particularly the thirst, for the heat of the sun was intense. He wished fervently for the cooling rain of the night before.

Sunset came, however, and with it a soft, cool wind. Skippy welcomed it, but hated the gray light of approaching twilight that obliterated the deep blue clouds. It seemed to spell doom to him and he cried out in despair. If daylight had not brought rescue what hope was there left for another long night?

His hopes sprang up afresh, however, and he conceived the idea of tying to the bell a long length of rope which he found in the bottom of the boat. In this manner, he could ring it constantly just by pulling the rope which required little exertion on his part. By dusk he was feeling too sick to either stand or sit up.

He entered his second night at sea both hopeful and despairing. Every doleful clang from the bell brought him hope but in the following silence it would quickly vanish and he would sink in depths of despair. Then with his fast-ebbing strength he would pull hopefully at the rope again.

EVERY DOLEFUL CLANG FROM THE BELL BROUGHT SKIPPY HOPE.

And so the bell tolled on through the long night hours.

***

CHAPTER XV

RESCUED

A few hours before dawn a long, trim, high-powered motor boat cut through the placidly rolling waves. Its motor was so muffled that it emitted no more than a low droning sound and could be heard for only a short distance, despite the fact that it had been let out to full speed.

Besides the man at the wheel the boat carried six men, three standing fore and three aft. One of the men aft half lounged over the coaming and his broad shoulders and large, amiable face all but filled the stern of the boat. The spray constantly swept over his big, dangling hands and the salt moisture struck at his tanned cheeks but he seemed not to notice. His entire attention, like that of his comrades, was centered on the grayish black horizon; his eyes seemed to miss nothing, yet there was an abstracted look in them that the man at the wheel did not fail to notice.

"Whadja hear, Big Joe?" he asked quietly.

The big man nodded his head without moving his body.

"'Tis that buoy," he said absently. "Sure and she's goin' a great rate for such a calm, me lad. Even in pretty bad storms I niver knowed Flint's buoy to be ringin' like that."

"Flint's?" queried another of the men, interested.

Big Joe Tully smiled reminiscently.

"And why not? 'Tis what most o' Flint's men called it. 'Tis a buoy at the intrance to Kennedy's Channel and 'tis a bad spot, if iver there was wan. Ye niver know how the tide's goin' to act. 'Tis like a colleen what can't make up her mind, and she's not to be trusted, so nobody goes by that way. Besides, 'tis a long way round past the Hook. Anyways, the ould boss took advantage o' that place and we used to meet some o' his best customers there and unload the stuff to thim."

"Not a bad idea takin' us by there for an eyeful, hey, Tully?" suggested the man at the wheel. "Long's you've decided on playin' ball with us, since we squared that case 'gainst you, we might as well take your tips. Seems like a wise mug like ol' Flint never made no mistakes. He got rich an' the law never got him so if *he* picked out a spot like this buoy, he must 'a' known what he was doin'. Mebbe it'll be a pretty good spot for our customers too?"

They all laughed at this, but Big Joe Tully merely smiled and glanced down at the compass.

"Sure and ould Flint made his mistakes and plenty," he said in his soft, deep voice. "He made mistakes whin he didn't watch out that the coppers didn't take the scows o' men what was workin' for his racket. And he made a mistake whin he stuck Toby Dare with a piece o' junk. I guess he thought he'd be puttin' me on me uppers where I'd be goin' back and beg him for work."

"He got knocked off fust, didn't he, Big Joe?" laughed the man at the wheel.

"That he did. 'Tis too bad he couldn't 'a' lived to see how quick I connected with you guys."

"It's too bad he couldn' lived anyways," said another of the men, "'cause that poor guy Dare wouldn't be in the can then. Anyhow I don't think he knocked him off. I think he'd liked to 'cause Flint give him a lousy break, but I believe what he said in court that some other guy beat him to it."

"I know lots o' guys what were layin' for ould Flint," said Big Joe. "Sure he'd been dead a dozen times if iverywan what had it in for him, did what they said they'd like to. That's why they won't be holdin' poor Toby."

"All the same, they *are* holdin' poor Toby," said the man at the wheel. "He was sentenced late yesterday afternoon for twenty years to life an' by this time he's hittin' the hay in the big house, that's what."

"And didn't ye hear!" said another. "His kid, Skippy, ain't been seen since he had a talk with Marty Skinner aboard the *Apollyon*. Poor kid, he went there to plead for his old man, the paper says, and that hardshell Skinner wouldn't give him a break, I guess. The second mate told a reporter that the kid left the yacht in a rush, hopped in his kicker and beat it for the Hook. Guess he thought as long as he couldn't do nothin' for Toby, he'd get away somewhere and try an' fergit. Well, that's life."

Big Joe Tully clenched his knotted, hairy fists.

"Sufferin' swordfish!" he said. "Poor Toby! And that poor kid! 'Tis a howlin' shame, so 'tis."

"Know 'em?" asked the man at the wheel.

"I oughta—I worked 'longside o' Toby doin' Flint's jobs night after night, so I did. A whiter guy than Toby niver lived. He ain't old— thirty-four or so. Got married whin he was a kid and his wife died. He's crazy 'bout that kid o' his, Skippy. 'Tis what makes me feel bad." Big Joe looked down at the compass once more. "North, northeast," he said to the man at the wheel. "We oughta be at Flint's buoy in twinty minutes. There's the light from the Hook."

They watched intently the great sweeping arc of light swinging over the smoothly rolling water. The motor boat plunged north, then northeast and in Big Joe Tully's eyes was a thoughtful, puzzled expression, the closer they got to the buoy.

"D'ye say there ain't somethin' spooky 'bout the way that bell's ringin'?" he asked his comrades. "Did ye iver hear a bell on a buoy ring like that without stoppin'? 'Tain't natural, 'cause...."

Just then he caught a glimpse of the little kicker bobbing merrily alongside the buoy.

***

CHAPTER XVI

RIVER PEOPLE

"An' when I sees ye layin' in the bottom o' that kicker, I'd swore I was seein' things so I would," Big Joe Tully was saying. "Lucky I gets it in me noodle that somethin's wrong the way that bell keeps ringin'."

The shanty of the *Minnie M. Baxter* was bright with the light of mid-morning. The floor had been scrubbed almost to whiteness, the table was laid with a soft Turkey red cloth and the lamp looked shiny and clean. Skippy's feverish eyes took it all in before he turned on his pillow.

"I felt so sick, I didn't exactly know it was you," he said weakly. "I heard voices, but I couldn't think what it was all about. All I'd thought all night was that I hadda keep on ringin' the bell."

"Sure, kid, and ye rang it!" said Big Joe with a light laugh.

"An' you sure saved me," Skippy smiled in return. "Gee, it was lucky you came that way, huh? Where'd you been?"

Big Joe lighted a cigarette and puffed on it before answering.

"Sure an' just puttin' the big eye on some new location for a new racket," he said softly. "I got six men with me."

"Is it—is it gonna be straight?" Skippy asked.

"Nah," Big Joe laughed. "Who'll be straight in the Basin and live like a human bein'? As 'tis, what they got? They're all doin' the higher-up's dirty work; but *me*, I ain't so foolish even if ould Flint tipped off the coppers and they grab me scow. I got a little money and I'll

                                        Among the River Pirates

work this new racket and make lots more. The doctor says ye've got a pretty weak lung so ye need a month in bed and the best o' food. Well, sufferin' swordfish, we'll dig up the dough so's ye'll be fat an' sassy 'fore Toby comes out."

Skippy's eyes lighted up.

"Gee, Mr. Tully, it must be costin' an awful lotta money for a lawyer to appeal the case, huh?"

Big Joe waved a large hand deprecatingly.

"Forget it, Skippy. Ain't I doin' it for a good friend and ain't I doin' it so's ye won't see Toby in the can for twinty years or more? Don't ye be worryin' 'bout the dough, me lad. I made it with the scow easy. Now it'll do you and Toby some good, so 'twill."

"Gee whiz," breathed the boy gratefully. "It's too much for you to do for Pop and me 'cause we can't pay it back—*never!*"

"That's why ye gotta be forgettin' it!" Tully protested. "I ain't got nobody to spend it on, kid, so I might's well spend it on you and Toby. I'd only leave it to ye in me will whin I died!" He laughed loudly. "Now'll we be good friends, kid?"

Skippy had to fight back the tears before he smiled.

"Gee, *sure!* Gee, I like you an awful lot, Mis—"

"Cut out the *Mister*, kid! Big Joe's me monicker, and nothin' else. Now anythin' more on that big mind o' yourn?"

Skippy nodded hesitantly.

"Gee—gee whiz," he stammered, "I just was thinkin' wouldn't it be nice if you had enough money so you didn't have to go into any crooked rackets for a while, huh? Gee, I'd like to think you didn't have to do it, honest I would, Big Joe! Maybe I'll be able to go to work when I get strong and I'll be able to help then, huh? Maybe we can live on clean, honest money like Pop wanted me to, huh? Besides, the money you're helpin' Pop and me with is kind of from when you were runnin' your barge straight, isn't it?"

Big Joe got up from his chair, went over to the table and ground out his cigarette stub in an ash tray. Then he came back and leaning over Skippy's bunk, he rumpled the boy's hair playfully.

"'Tis a funny lad ye be, Skippy. But I s'pose ye be gettin' it from Toby. He was always agin doin' Flint's work. Said he wouldn't 'a' started it if he hadn't been takin' care o' ye so much daytimes whin ye was sick with that throat business."

"Pop was always honest inside, that shows it," said Skippy proudly.

Big Joe smiled.

"Anyways ye're right about me runnin' me barge straight the first year," he said vehemently. "I did." Then: "So ye want me on the level? Well, we'll be seein' about that but we ain't goin' to starve I'll be tellin' ye, so I will."

Skippy's eyes were shining.

"You'll get along if people can see you're tryin' to be honest, that's what Pop said."

"Sufferin' swordfish, kid," said Big Joe. "Be quittin' thinkin' 'bout anythin' now 'ceptin' gettin' better. And no more talk about work when ye're better. Sufferin' swordfish, ye ain't nothin' but skin and bones, the doctor said! Ye're as pale as a ghost, too. Eggs, milk and chicken soup is what ye need and what ye'll be gettin'."

"Who'll fix 'em?" Skippy asked, chuckling weakly.

"Our nixt door neighbor on the *Dinky O. Cross*," Big Joe said. "She's a right nice woman, kid—Mrs. Duffy, and as soon as she sees us carryin' ye in she said it milted her heart. So we put a plank across to her scow and she come in here and did 'bout iverythin' 'fore the doctor come. I give her the dough for the things and she's cookin' thim now."

"She's a—she's one of the river people, huh? Like *you*, Big Joe?" Skippy asked wondering.

"Like you and me, Skippy me boy," answered Big Joe, nodding his head. "She's one o' our people, the kind what helps their own whin there's trouble."

 Among the River Pirates

Skippy shut his eyes to visualize the stern, cold visage of Marty Skinner. Hadn't he talked of river people as if they were all of a kind? Hadn't he said they were all crooks and criminals?

Big Joe had put him in that category of river people, he who had never disobeyed a law in his young life! He resented it and wanted to say so, but his better judgment prevailed against it and he decided to wait and see what kind of people these river people of Brown's Basin really were. Certainly if they were all like Big Joe Tully, Skinner had much to learn.

It was the buxom Mrs. Duffy who decided it, some moments later. She came in like the fresh morning breeze from the inlet, clean-aproned and smiling, laden with soup and eggnog and a wealth of bright cretonne tucked under her generous arm.

"Cretonne curtains for thim little windows, bhoy," she said breathlessly. "Mr. Tully give me the money for 'em an' I made 'em up 'fore I come over. It'll seem more like home to ye in Brown's Basin whin ye see 'em from the outside. The inlet's dismal enough, so 'tis, without starin' at it through bare, dirty winders; ain't I right, Mr. Tully?"

"Guess so," Big Joe answered a little abashed. "Women folks know more about thim things, but even me, I be likin' that bright stuff flutterin' around a winder. Ye got the soup an' everythin'?"

Mrs. Duffy's smile was vast and it swept from Big Joe to the wan-looking Skippy.

"Ye'll pick up, so ye will, or me and Mr. Tully'll be to blame, Skippy," she said heartily.

Skippy almost choked with gratitude. He tried to speak, but could only think that these were river people—his people! Big Joe, who was spending a lot of money so that his father might have another chance for freedom and who would spare no expense to nurse him back to health. And Mrs. Duffy, who was bringing cheer into the shanty of the *Minnie M. Baxter* and who seemed to care so much that he get well!

River people? Skinner didn't know what he was talking about! He, Skippy Dare, was proud to be one of the river people.

***

CHAPTER XVII

MUGS

Many delightful weeks Skippy spent after he was up and around. Day after day, he and Big Joe roamed the length and breadth of the river, and often they went down the bay and across to some unfrequented beach where they swam and fished to their hearts' content.

Skippy soon showed the effects of his healthful life and Mrs. Duffy's fine cooking. He was browned from head to foot and his flat chest had expanded two inches. And what was more, he had learned to triumph over tears.

That in itself was a great achievement, for he had great need to practice self-control during the fall and the winter following. The gods themselves seemed to have cast sorrowful glances over the *Minnie M. Baxter* and Skippy's mettle was tried to the breaking point sometimes, yet always he came up smiling. Very often it was a poignant smile, the kind that pierced Big Joe Tully's almost invulnerable heart and set him to doing all sorts of extravagant things so that he might see the pain effaced from the boy's face and hear him laugh happily.

That was why on the evening of Toby's retrial, Big Joe left the shanty of the *Minnie M. Baxter* in awkward haste. He had left Skippy smiling a smile so poignant that he could bear it no longer.

"Big Joe," the boy said when they were dawdling over the most luxurious meal that Tully's money could buy, "it was most like throwin' money away, huh? They don't wanta let Pop get out, I guess. They can't find the man that really did it and they've gotta have somebody so I

                                   Among the River Pirates

s'pose they think it might's well be my Pop. Now he *will* be in for life on account of the way they tripped him up in his answers. Gee, how could he remember word for word what he said at his first trial? People don't remember word for word 'bout things like that. Poor Pop was so nervous I got chills down my back."

"Don't ye be gettin' down, kid," Tully protested; "'tis not sayin' we're licked till they turn down an appeal. We got some more dough."

"So much money," said Skippy with a note of wonder in his high-pitched voice. "Gee, Big Joe, you've spent so much on Pop an' me already. Now you wanta spend the last you got! Gee whiz, I can't let you—*I can't!* Much as I wanta see Pop free. It ain't fair lettin' you spend all your hard-earned money...."

Tully had long since learned that he could not lie to Skippy.

"Sure an' this last coin ain't hard-earned, kid," he said not a little abashed. "So ye see 'cause it ain't, it might's well be used for springin' your old man."

"All right, if you say it like that," said Skippy with a slightly reproving smile. Suddenly he squared his shoulders; then: "Anyway, next to Pop, Big Joe, I like you best. Gee, ain't you been just like Pop even! So I don't care if that money's not so straight, but d'ye think it'll be lucky for Pop? Sometimes I wonder if crooked money ain't hard luck in the end. Maybe when you're broke you can start over clean?"

"We'll see what the breaks'll be bringin' this winter, kid," Big Joe had mumbled. "We'll see, so we will."

And it was Skippy's answering smile that drove Big Joe off the barge for a few hours. When he returned late in the evening, he had a fluffy sort of bundle in his big arms and an expansive smile on his face.

"Three guesses what's in me arms," he said with a mischievous wink, standing half in and half out of the doorway.

"Is it dead or alive?" Skippy asked chuckling.

"'Tis the liveliest little guy ye ever see." Big Joe stooped over and released the fluffy bundle from his arms and presently an Airedale pup put its four young and rather unsteady legs on the shanty floor.

Skippy laughed out loud. He twisted his hands together in a gesture of delight, then got to his knees and coaxed the puppy to him.

"It's got brown eyes like a reg'lar angel," he said.

"An' brown legs like the divil," Big Joe laughed; "the divil for runnin' into mischief. The man what I bought him from said he was a son-of-a-sufferin' swordfish for runnin' an' chewin'. But he'll be gettin' better as he gets older, so he will. Ain't he got the cute little mug though, kid!"

Skippy looked up with shining eyes, then drew the puppy up to him.

"Big Joe, that's his name—it's a swell name for him! Mug—*Mugs*, huh? With that funny little face he couldn't be called anything else."

"Sure, sure, kid. Anythin' ye say. Mugs it'll be, so 'twill." He coughed. "And will he be makin' ye happy now, kid?"

"*Happy!* Big Joe, Mugs'll make me happy 'cause you bought him to make me laugh. Gee, gee...." Skippy swallowed his emotion. "What for do you do so much, Big Joe?" he asked naïvely. "Gee—*why?*"

"'Cause ye be such a nice kid, so ye be," the man answered, rumpling Skippy's straight hair. "Ye kind o' get under a guy's skin—ye do that. Ye seem to be needin' somebody for to look after ye, so ye do, an' with Toby not about it might's well be me." He laughed nervously. "Besides I ain't got nobody else at all, at all, kid, an' even a tough guy like me does be needin' company, so he does."

Skippy hugged the puppy gratefully and he was so overwhelmed by Tully's generosity that he could not speak. Never, he thought, did a boy have a friend like Big Joe!

His cup of happiness would have been filled to the brim and his father been released that day. But here again, Big Joe, like an angel of mercy, was making a last supreme effort to bring his father back to him. It seemed impossible that such gigantic effort could fail to bring a joyous result and he told Tully so.

"An' when Pop gets out," he said in conclusion, "I bet he'll never

Among the River Pirates

forget what you've done an' all, Big Joe. Even now he don't forget it. He said it's so gloomy and strict in prison that he's sad all the time, 'specially 'cause he was so used to roamin' all over the river free. Gee, he said the feller what really killed Mr. Flint was a coward 'cause he must know how it's keepin' Pop an' me away from each other an' he said he could almost kill him for doin' that alone."

"There, now, the ould man'll be gettin' out!" said Tully vehemently. "My last grand'll do it, I be tellin' ye! See if it don't! Now ye ain't goin' to start worryin' all over 'bout Toby now, are ye? An' me gettin' ye Mugs so's to make it aisier like for ye."

Skippy looked at the puppy sliding over the floor on his gawky legs. He laughed.

"Mugs makes up for an awful lot, Big Joe, but nobody could make up for Pop," he said wistfully. "I never told Pop, 'cause he'd think it sounded silly, but I love him. You know, like I guess girls feel only they show it an' talk about it, but I don't. I couldn't. But I'm just tellin' you like a secret—see? I get a funny pain in my heart when I'm not seein' Pop an' it gets awful bad when I think maybe he won't ever get out of prison." Then at the sight of Big Joe's frowning countenance, he added: "But it's like I said, Big Joe, I like you almost as much as Pop. An' now you've bought me Mugs—gee, how much'd you pay for him, huh?"

"'Tis nothin'," said Big Joe smiling softly; "a coupla bucks. 'Course, they cost a little more thin just muts, but the man at the dog place said thim Airedales be great for protectin' kids so I think maybe he'd be good for ye nights when I might be out with the boys. He'll be comp'ny anyways."

A little later, when Big Joe was having a good-night smoke alone on the deck, he took out of his pocket a piece of paper, and in the light gleaming from the cabin windows he glanced at it curiously. It was a receipt for one Airedale puppy; price, one hundred and fifty dollars.

He smiled, shrugged his powerful shoulders and tearing the paper into bits let it drop in the inlet. Then he turned his trousers' pockets outward and laughed ruefully.

"Broke," he said half aloud. "Sure and 'tis aisy come, aisy go. And now for to be gettin' some more dough. The kid'll be needin' it so——" He shrugged as if getting money was the least of his troubles.

***

Among the River Pirates

CHAPTER XVIII

BAD NEWS

Skippy had food and plenty of it during the next month. Big Joe saw to that though it kept him away from the barge many hours at night, hours when he lived in mortal fear that the boy would develop a "bad throat" and be seriously sick before he could get back.

Skippy's "bad throat" had become a veritable bugaboo to Tully and though he had no definite idea of what it was, the fear of its recurrence stalked every hour that he spent away from the boy. And when he did return he would tiptoe into the silent shanty and up to the boy's bunk, sighing with relief to find him sleeping quietly. Then, when he had made sure there was no sign of the pinched look and feverish cheek, he would climb into his own bunk with a light on his face that would have surprised his rough comrades.

Skippy saw this light on Tully's face one early morning. He saw it from under half-opened lids and it made him glad until he noticed the quick look of concern that passed over the man's tanned brow.

"What's up, Big Joe?" he asked anxiously.

"So it's awake ye be?" Big Joe returned nervously. "Well now I was just lookin' and seem' if ye was all right. Sure an' the weather's gittin' cold and all and I got wonderin' how the throat was. I bought a new stove what'll give ye lots o' heat—it's comin' in the mornin'."

"Gee whiz!" Skippy said gratefully, then: "You sorta looked worried."

Big Joe turned his back and started to undress.

"I've got to be tellin' ye sometime, kid—I—listen...."

"You've heard about Pop, huh?" Skippy sat up.

"Yes—they...."

"They what?" said Skippy anxiously.

"They turned down the appeal. But don't be takin' on about it, Skippy. Sure an' next year we'll be diggin' up new evidence. Now...."

"I ain't gonna take on, Big Joe, honest I ain't," said Skippy bravely. "On accounta you I ain't. You been so good—all the money you spent tryin' to get Pop free. An' now—well, maybe if I don't hope about it sumpin'll happen, sometime."

"Sure now that's bein' a good kid, takin' it so aisy like. We'll be tryin' agin like I said. Some time Marty Skinner'll get over his crazy notion that iverybody in Brown's Basin's agin him and that Toby did the job. Sure he hates iverybody here so much I hear he's got Buck Flint to agree to buy the whole inlet. And thin he'll be drivin' us squatters out, so he will."

"But he can't do that!" Skippy protested indignantly. "He can't drive me outa the *Minnie M. Baxter* 'cause it's Pop's home—gee, the only home we got. I gotta stay here till—well, when I leave it, I'll know I ain't got any hope that he'll come back."

"And don't I be knowin' how ye feel, kid? But if Skinner's put it in Buck Flint's head that the inlet's a good buy and the deal goes through, he'll be orderin' us out and we'll be likin' it. Buck ain't a bad egg, but Skinner's runnin' the works and what he says goes, so it does. Now if he tells us to beat it I'm wonderin' who'll be towin' a barge out o' this mud whin she's settled. Why, it'd take a derrick, so it would, an' even then it'd be a chance."

Skippy was deeply affected by this news. He could not sleep because of it and long after Big Joe was snoring comfortably he rolled and tossed in his bunk. Then, after a time, he thought of what Tully had said about the barges being too deeply settled in the mud to get them out, and he was so curious about it that he got up to see for himself.

He bundled himself up and slipped out onto the deck in the cold, damp air of an early fall morning. It was not yet dawn but the deep black of night had gone and Brown's Basin lay silent in a dark gray mist.

Among the River Pirates

Skippy leaned far over aft where the *Minnie M. Baxter* was settled deepest in the mud. Up forward, the slinking waters of the inlet gurgled plaintively against the keel at high tide. Big Joe was right, he decided with sinking heart; it would take a derrick and more to pull the barge out of her muddy berth.

As he started to step back he noticed a tarpaulin to his right which seemed to be covering some bulky objects. Something that Big Joe had brought aboard, he thought, and curiously he raised one end of it. One glimpse told him enough.

They were stolen ships' supplies, things that his father had told him a river pirate could easily dispose of to some unscrupulous ship captain. Skippy knew instantly how they had come there and he turned on his heel and had started back for the shanty when a searchlight suddenly fell full upon him.

He crouched out of its glare and needed but to look hastily up the inlet to see that it was the police boat bearing down upon the *Minnie M. Baxter.*

***

CHAPTER XIX

DANGER

Feverishly, Skippy set to work and pushed the stolen goods overboard piece by piece. Most of them floated but a moment, then sank out of sight, and the rest floated at a safe enough distance from the oncoming launch to escape the eyes of the police.

FEVERISHLY SKIPPY PUSHED THE STOLEN GOODS OVERBOARD.

When the last piece had been disposed of he rushed to the shanty, awakened Big Joe and told him what he had done.

"'Tis a good boy ye be, Skippy," he praised. "Sure th' bulls give me a chase tonight so they did and I couldn' unload the goods on me customer so I brought thim here till tomorrow night. Ye're a broth of a lad to be droppin' thim over, so ye be."

"Sh!" said Skippy, frightened. "Ain't that them boardin' us now?" He got out of his clothes and back into his bunk.

They listened in silence while the soft tramp of feet came along the deck. Skippy had reason to remember another terrible occasion when the police boat had come to take his father. He had thought then that it was only for a day.

He had only Big Joe now, his only friend in a singularly callous world. Would the law take him too? He couldn't bear it—he wouldn't bear it! He would like and protect Big Joe even if he was a murderer, the police wouldn't take the one thing he had left!

They knocked insistently and Big Joe padded to the door, barefooted and feigning complete surprise. He invited them in, hurried ponderously to the rickety table and lighted the lamp. Mugs growled ominously.

The officers told Tully that a certain warehouse had been broken into that night. The watchman who had surprised the intruder thought he had recognized Big Joe Tully.

"Tonight?" Skippy piped up from his bunk. "It ain't so 'cause Big Joe's been here takin' care of me since noon. I got one of my bad throats again an' he wouldn't go out 'cause I was feelin' so bad."

Who of the river front police hadn't heard of Skippy Dare's bad throat? None that had patrolled the harbor during the past four months. Hadn't it been because of his frail boy that Toby Dare had fought his prison sentence so hard? The papers had been full of it too.

"So the throat's cutting up again, eh Skippy?" asked Inspector Jones. He was the same man who had taken Toby away from his son.

Skippy, always a bit wan looking when he lay in his bunk, looked more wan than ever then. His pallor was not simulated; it was terribly real, for he was not only frightened at the prospect of losing Big Joe; he was frightened because of the barefaced lie he had just told—the first in his life.

"I always gotta be careful of my throat, Mister," he said to the officer when the worst of his emotion had passed. "'Specially when it gets cold. Sometimes I get fever right away an' the doctor told Big Joe the last time that I gotta right away have attention."

"Sure and the lad's right," Big Joe interposed with genuine feeling in his voice, "he's got only me to be lookin' after him now."

"What you doing for a living, Big Joe?" asked the officer a little pointedly.

Big Joe stifled a yawn and sat down on a chair.

"Me?" he asked innocently. "Ye mean what'll I do when the money I saved from me barge gives out, is it? With the way Flint blackballed me 'fore he died, I guess I'll have to be workin' out o' the bay next summer, so I do."

"Got enough for you and the kid till next summer?" the officer persisted.

"Sure and 'tis lucky I have, the way things be," answered Big Joe.

The officer leveled his eyes at Tully.

"For the kid's sake, watch your step, Big Joe," he said with a warning note. "For the kid's sake...."

Skippy couldn't believe they had gone. It seemed too good to be true, and in order to reassure him, Big Joe put something around him and went out on deck to see that the launch had actually gone.

"Sure she's aisy out to the river by this time," he assured Skippy when he came back. He lighted a cigarette and sat down. "Now was that a close shave I'll be askin'," he exclaimed. "And I can be thankin' ye for it, kid. I never expected thim to come stealin' up on us here, no, I didn't."

"See it don't pay, Big Joe!" Skippy said gently. He seemed spent with the great strain. "People know a big guy like you anywheres an' besides like I say, it don't pay anyhow. Gee, if you can't get honest work 'cause Flint blackballed you then I gotta work myself. I can get a job as office boy in a warehouse. I bet I can!"

"Nix, kid, nix, ye ain't well enough," Big Joe protested hotly. "Besides I don't niver take things from folks what are hard up, Skippy. I——"

"Lemme try it, Big Joe, huh? I'm better now'n I been in a long time, so lemme try it! I'm not kickin' 'bout you. Gee, I can see how it is now. Even Pop once told me how hard it was for a blackballed man to get back along the river. You spent all your money on Pop an' me an' we hadda eat an' live, so what was you gonna do! I shoulda known before that your money couldn't last forever—gee! All you've done for me, Big Joe—lemme try!"

Tully was still protesting at daylight, but Skippy, having made up his mind, fell peacefully to sleep with the dog tucked snugly under his outstretched arm. Big Joe sat watching them until long after the sun came up.

Among the River Pirates

"Sure and the kid lied for me," he said as he climbed back into his bunk. "Sure and that nice kid lied for me—*me!*"

And as his large features settled in slumber, they looked strangely troubled.

***

CHAPTER XX

A JOB

S kippy left the barge noiselessly that morning and did not return until six o'clock in the evening. Consequently, Big Joe spent a troubled day, waiting and hoping and fearing. When he saw the boy crossing the plank from the *Dinky O. Cross*, he hurried to the door.

"And where have ye been, Skippy?" he called anxiously. "Here and ye been havin' me crazy wonderin' if ye'd run away!"

Skippy laughed and greeted Mugs who seemed to be growing by the minute. Then he swung energetically into the shanty and sat down to a hot supper that Mrs. Duffy had faithfully sent over.

"Guess what, Big Joe?"

"Sure and ye'll not be for quittin' me 'cause o' what happened last night?" Big Joe returned trying not to sound anxious.

"I should say not. Whad'ye think I am? I ain't yeller, Big Joe. Besides I like you too much. What I wanta say is, I got a job."

Tully frowned.

"It ain't gonna be hard," Skippy assured him. "I'm the new office boy at the Central Warehouse an' I'll get ten bucks a week. So now you needn't be scareda cops."

Tully smiled in spite of himself. "My now, ain't that just fine. Ain't that just fine, kid. But do ye be knowin' who's boss o' the Central?"

"No. Who?"

"Marty Skinner, actin' as Buck Flint's agent, no less."

"Well, he can see then that my Pop brought me up honest an' hard workin'," said Skippy after a moment's surprise.

"Sure, to be sure and he can that, but shiverin' swordfish, don't ye be goin' on expectin' too much from him, kid. D'ye be thinkin' he's wise ye be on the payroll?"

"No."

"Well, now, just ye be waitin' till he is. Just ye be...."

Skippy did not have long to wait. He had completed his first week's work in the Central Warehouse when one day he heard a hushed voice pass around the awesome news that "the boss" was coming.

Skinner recognized Skippy as soon as he stepped into the room. There were a few questions asked and Skippy trudged back to the *Minnie M. Baxter* that night with a heavy heart.

Big Joe was all sympathy.

"And what was he sayin' to ye, kid?"

"He wanted to know how I come to get a job there," Skippy answered dolefully. "Wanted to know how I had nerve enough an' said I was there as a spotter for my father's gang probably. An' before he finished he said it was lucky there hadn't been a robbery there or he'd handed me right over to the police then an' there. *Me*—me that ain't done him a bitta harm an' that wouldn't! Gee, Big Joe, ain't it enough that he helped put Pop where he is? Can't he see how *I* am?"

"None o' 'em can see anythin', kid," Big Joe answered, bitterly. "That's the trouble with me and Toby and every man in this Basin. Sure 'tis 'cause the likes o' Skinner can't see. They don't even give us a chance, they don't 'cause we're river folks. They tell us so much that we're crooked that we wind up that way whither we want to or not, so we do. They make us be crooked. And now they be startin' in on you, kid. 'Tis a dirty shame, so 'tis."

"I'll get some other place," Skippy was defiant. "They're not gonna make me crooked when I don't wanna be."

"Skippy, kid," thought Tully from the depths of his river front wisdom, "I ain't so sure, I ain't so sure." But what he said was: "Sure and that they'll not, Skippy me boy, that they'll not."

***

CHAPTER XXI

WHAT NEXT?

Weary week after weary week passed for Skippy until the winter months had come and gone. March arrived, cold, blustery and disappointing, for he hadn't yet been able to hold a job longer than it took his employers to find out just who their office boy was. And as gossip spreads quickly along the river front, the discouraged boy seldom drew more than a few days' pay at a time.

He had learned upon being dismissed from his last job the reason why employers had no use for his services. He demanded to know.

"Is it 'cause my father's in prison?" he asked wistfully. "'Cause if it is nobody is fair in the world. You've heard, I bet, that lots of innocent people are in jail so can't you believe maybe my father could be one of them? And anyway, does that prove that I'm...."

The employer, thus confronted, protested.

"No," he said in that self-righteous tone that was beginning to wear on Skippy's nerves, "we think that you, yourself, mean to be honest but we know that you can't hold out long against such home conditions as the Basin offers. A wage such as a boy like you with your limited education can earn isn't enough to provide you with all you want. And sooner or later, your association with a person like Big Joe Tully will have its effect on you."

"My Pop was gonna send me to school so's I could get educated," Skippy protested, "but anyway I'm honest an' I'm gonna stay honest, no matter what you think. Besides, Big Joe's tried to live straight all this winter for my sake, but are you an' everybody else I've tried to work for tryin' to help him? No, nobody won't even give him a job so he can stay straight. An' now you won't let me stay 'cause I live with him, because you're afraid...."

"My dear boy," the employer interposed patronizingly, "can you blame us? Tully has served a jail sentence for robbing our warehouses. How can we be certain that he won't do it again? Or that he won't use your position of trust in our offices to learn more easily what goods we have in our warehouses that he can steal? What assurance can you give us that he don't do that when he gets tired treading the straight and narrow path? None. Absolutely none! No, we warehouse owners have been too long aware that it is you thieving river people who are responsible for our tremendous losses every year. And so we maintain that, once a thief, always a thief!"

Skippy was wounded and bitter. His full, generous lips curled sardonically.

"Then it ain't any use to try to make you understand," he said bravely. "You warehouse people complain that we're thieves an' you make us thieves just like you're tryin' to make me one by keepin' me outa jobs so's I can't make an honest livin'. An' anyway, if the only way I could hold a job is to quit Big Joe then I won't do it! I'd rather *be* a thief, yes I would! He saved my life and he's helped my Pop ... oh, what's the use!"

He slammed the door behind him and rushed home to find Big Joe with his faithful, smiling face. Plank after plank he hurried over, connecting the barges, and at last he crossed the deck of the *Dinky O. Cross*, waved a greeting to the smiling Mrs. Duffy and whistled for Mugs when he reached the plank of the *Minnie M. Baxter*.

"And have ye lost the job, kid?" Big Joe asked when he entered the shanty.

"My last job, Big Joe," the boy answered smiling ruefully. "You were right about 'em—there ain't one that'll gimme a chance. Even you who ain't always been honest yourself did more than that! You let me try at least. They know more about you than I did—they know you served time."

"Sure and that's why they're blackballin' ye, is it? 'Cause ye're stickin' with me?" His bland face looked dark and ominous. Then as he glanced at the boy's wistful countenance, his expression softened: "I'm tellin' ye the truth, kid, whin I say that they railroaded me, so they did—I was startin' in honest like you. Office boy. Thin one night the warehouse was robbed and next mornin' they accused me o' workin' with the gang—tippin' 'em off. 'Cause I'd been seen 'round with one o' the guys what was caught. I got a year, I did, and didn't have a chance. When I come out I was blackballed and Ol' Flint took me under. Sufferin' swordfish, sure and I've tried twice now to travel on the up and up. When I first got my barge and now. And 'tis no use, 'tis no use."

"Seems that way," Skippy murmured, disconsolate. "Now I ain't gonna try. I'm gonna live an' eat like other fellers my age. I wanta go to the movies an' take things up to Pop when I go to see him. Gee, already he's startin' to write to me that the food's bad up at the big house. So I gotta help him have a little sumpin' to smile at if he's gonna be there the rest of his life! An' I gotta have money to go to see him—I gotta see him! If they won't lemme earn it honest—*what else*? Like the man said, I don't know enough to work anywheres else."

"And ye'll be wantin' to quit me, kid? Ye'll be wantin' to go away and start over where they don't know 'bout river people and all?" Big Joe's anxiety was pathetic.

"I'm afraid of places too far away from the river," Skippy admitted. "I guess I got the river in me like Pop, huh? I ain't got nerve enough to break away. Besides I sorta promised Pop I'd stay by the *Minnie M. Baxter*. S'pose just by a lucky break the governor pardons Pop some day, huh? He's paid good money for this barge an' it's the only home he's got. Besides, I don't wanta quit you, Big Joe—*I couldn't*!"

And Skippy's decision stood until Brown's Basin was no more....

***

CHAPTER XXII

BIG JOE'S IDEA

In May, Big Joe conceived a brilliant idea for making a living. He came into the shanty of the barge with it one balmy noon, for it was embodied in a large canvas bag which he carried in his big outstretched hand.

"Sure and now we be goin' to eat, kid, and we be goin' to live high, and ye be goin' to do all the things ye' want for Toby," he said chuckling.

"Stealin'?" Skippy asked, looking worried and wan. "As hard up as we been, Big Joe, I can't stand for sneakin' down the river at night an' climbin' into warehouse windows. Gee, Pop'd feel fierce if we was caught an' I was put in reform school or sumpin' like that!"

"And d'ye be thinkin' I ain't carin' no more for ye than seein' ye grabbed for somethin' like that, me boy? Kid, I been thinkin' and thinkin' o' some way for us to be gettin' by—some way that no copper could catch us up on. And if they iver should 'twon't be you what'd be holdin' the bag—'twill be me, 'cause I'm the one what'll do the trick. Do you catch on?"

"What trick, Big Joe?"

"'Tis the stuff I got in this bag, kid," answered Tully softly. "'Tis ground carbon and whin it's poured in with oil it raises the divil with thim nice engines in rich guys' boats up at the Riverview Yacht Club. From now on till the end o' summer they're takin' trips—see? Well, sure and Big Joe's got a good pal what looks out for the boats up there ... he's told beforehand what rich guy's goin' out in his boat, he

                                    Among the River Pirates

is ... my pal tells me and I go up there—see? Him and me edge aisy like towards the boat and whilst he's lookin' out the corners o' his eye that no one's comin', Big Joe uncovers the crank case and 'fore ye could say *scat*, I'm pourin' me little powder in the breather pipe and sure she's mixin' with the oil."

"An' what then?" Skippy asked, nervous, yet admiring Big Joe's ingenious idea.

Big Joe winked, then laughed.

"Sure, I pour the right amount o' this powder, kid," he said, "thin I beats it off quick and watch the rich guy start, so I do. If 'tis possible, me pal finds out where the guy's goin' so's I can beat it on ahead and circle his course so I come up on him by the time his ingine's dead—see?"

"The powder mixes through the oil an' up through the engine, huh?" Skippy asked fearfully. "Makes the engine go dead, huh?"

"Sure 'tis ground up like nobody's business, kid," Big Joe laughed. "An' I make sure o' puttin' in enough so's I'll be knowin' about where the ingine goes dead on thim. And thin I chug up to thim all innocent like and asks do they want help. *Do* they? Sure they must be towed back so I says I don't think I'm their man 'cause I'll be losin' business somewheres or other—see? And they're so anxious they'll be willin' to pay me price, so they will. And I gotta be paid for the loss o' me time!" He laughed heartily.

"I—I—gee, in a way that's worse than pulling a warehouse, Big Joe? It ain't so dangerous, but...."

"Kid, sure I thought ye'd be takin' on, but I can tell ye it ain't so bad at all, at all. I'll be pickin' out only thim what's payin' tin and twinty grand for their kickers! What's the cost to thim what throws away hundreds o' bucks at a time? And what's fifty or seventy-five bucks for to be payin' me for towin' thim back? Sure 'tis a drop in the bucket, says I. They'll niver be missin' it, kid. And we gotta live, you and me, and Toby's case's gotta go before the governor some day and that takes money too."

Skippy nodded and Big Joe noticed that the old pinched look had come back to his thin cheeks.

"Kid, ye can't be goin' on like this, you and me!" he pleaded. "Like I said 'tis only the big guys—guys what have the heavy sugar. We'll be layin' off the others and we'll be workin' the different clubs so nobody gets wise. Thim boat tenders'll go along for a little o' the split. So ye needn't be worryin' that we're takin' thim what can't afford it! Besides they're mostly rich warehouse guys that won't give you and me the chance for honest work. Sure and now ye won't be feelin' so bad about takin' it, will ye?"

That decided Skippy. Hunger and privation had dulled his conscience, embittered him against the warehouse owners and he was at last ready to strike back at his oppressors.

And strange to say, in contemplating the results of this stealthy enterprise, Skippy did not think of the food, nor the movies to which he could go. He was thinking instead that he would at last have the money to pay for his journey up to see his father. For a few golden moments the walls of the prison would fade away and Toby would imagine himself a free man. And all because of a breath of river air that his son would bring him in his smile.

And for that, Skippy was willing to forget that he hated dishonesty in any form.

***

Among the River Pirates

CHAPTER XXIII

ANOTHER JOB

It was early morning a few days later when Skippy and Tully set out on the first stage of their enterprise. The inlet was dark and shadowy, and the sweet soft breath of spring floated about their heads. In its wake, however, came the smell of mud and fish at low tide and the boy was glad to get out into the fresh salt air of the river.

"It's the only thing that makes me hate the inlet," he said to Big Joe as they turned up toward the yacht club. "I get feelin' choked, sorta— you know, sumpin' like I imagine people feel when they go to jail."

"Now don't ye be feelin' spooky," Tully admonished. "'Tain't the spirit for a job like this. Sure, there's somethin' 'bout mentionin' jail what gives me the creeps. So don't be thinkin' we'll be gettin' in any jams—'tis hard luck, so 'tis."

"I'm sorry, Big Joe," said Skippy contritely. "I—I didn't say it for that, honest, because even Pop can tell you how the inlet always made me feel like that. I'm all right when I'm up on the barge; it's only the inlet makes me feel that way. Just as soon as we strike the river I feel better."

"That's the talk, me boy. And I'm sorry for jumpin' on ye so quick. I thought ye was nervous 'bout this job, so I did."

"Aw, no," Skippy protested, but his quivering lip belied his words.

Tully did not see it, however, for he was intent on approaching the yacht club unobtrusively.

"Now if this ain't a good break," he said enthusiastically. "There's a party o' three goin' out on a two days' fishing trip at Snug Island.

She's called the *Minnehaha*, me pal tells me, and she's a baby. Twenty-six footer! Guy that owns her is Crosley."

"Crosley Warehouse where I worked last?" Skippy asked anxiously.

"Sure, and now don't that beat all! Little Old Lady Luck's playin' with us, kid! Sure 'tis a break to make him hand over his bucks or sink in Watson's Channel!"

"You wouldn't let 'em do that, Big Joe?" Skippy asked fearfully. "*You wouldn't!*"

"Nah, Big Joe ain't that hard hearted, much as I got it in for thim rich bugs. I'll just be lettin' thim think I'm doin' thim a favor not lettin' Watson's Channel close 'em in, so I will."

"Do you s'pose Mr. Crosley'll get wise we're doin' it a-purpose?" Skippy was beginning to weaken already.

"And how'll he be doin' that, I'm askin' ye? Me pal tipped me off they be due at dawn. We'll be there and gone a half hour afore they show up. So don't be startin' worryin', kid. Leave everythin' to Big Joe, as if ye didn't know nothin' 'bout the business at all, at all. You don't say nothin'. Be lookin' dumb if anybody talks to ye."

"I will," said Skippy, half-whimsically, and half-frightened. "I'll be *scared* dumb so you needn't worry that I'll get nervous an' give anythin' away—gee whiz!"

Big Joe laughed, then he said, "Awright, kid, D'ye be knowin' Skinner and Crosley be pals?"

"Gee!" said Skippy. "Now I know why I couldn't get a job. Skinner put 'em all wise, huh? Gee!"

They were silent after that and chugged steadily toward the yacht club. A ferry-boat was crossing far up the river and her lights blinked out over the dark water like a hundred evil eyes. Hundreds of boats anchored near shore bobbed up and down on the tide like a ghostly river army, and from the shore more lights winked down on them knowingly as if they knew their secret.

Among the River Pirates

They crept into the slip alongside the yacht club; Big Joe had shut off the motor. At a sign from him, Skippy dropped the anchor and without a word, he got out and crept across the float and onto the club grounds.

After the darkness hid him from view Skippy looked about, nervously. There was a little light gleaming from under the vast clubhouse porch and suddenly he saw Big Joe's ponderous figure pass under it. Presently, he halted and held out his hand to a man approaching him from the other direction.

Skippy sighed with relief and relaxed. At least Big Joe had met his comrade without accident. Besides, no one seemed to be about. He heard not a sound except the river lapping restlessly around the piling under the slip and the swish of anchored craft as they swayed on the tide.

It seemed to him that Big Joe was staying an interminable time, but as an actual fact, it was just seven minutes before he saw the man's bulky figure coming stealthily toward him.

Skippy weighed anchor without a sound and they pushed the kicker out of the slip with oars. A little distance below the club, Big Joe turned over his motor.

"Shiverin' swordfish, kid," he murmured with a chuckle, "all we do now is wait—wait so's Crosley can get 'bout as far as Watson's Channel. He'll be gettin' no further'n that—so he won't."

Skippy shivered a little and leaned over the coaming to watch for logs.

***

CHAPTER XXIV

ANOTHER RESCUE

As the moments wore on, Skippy felt meaner than ever. He tried to force himself to accept Big Joe's point of view, but it was difficult and more than once he wished he had not encouraged his good friend in this dubious enterprise.

They chugged into the bay and out of the awakening river traffic. Dawn had broken through and glimmerings of dancing light peeped over the horizon. An hour more and they would be in sight of Watson's Channel.

"We'll not be goin' straight for the Channel, we'll not," called Big Joe as if anticipating Skippy's fears. "We'll be layin' quite like below here a ways 'till the *Minnehaha* gets in the Channel. 'Tis a funny name, hey kid?"

"Mm," Skippy answered. "It's a Indian name, Big Joe—I think it means sumpin' like Laughing—Laughing sumpin'."

Big Joe's mirth knew no bounds.

"Sure and just about now *Minnie* ain't laughin', she ain't," he said. "'Tis us."

"Not me," Skippy said gloomily. "I won't laugh ... not till after."

An hour later they were chugging noisily toward Watson's Channel. The sun was glorious and the water glistened under its warm spring rays. Gulls frolicked about in the foaming spray and Skippy tried hard to believe there was nothing but peace in his busy mind.

Among the River Pirates

After a time they heard a distant sound, faint at first but growing louder within a few minutes. Tully grinned at Skippy's questioning face and nodded as the piercing note of a siren cut the silent sunlit air.

"Sure, and I wonder what that might be?" he said with mock-seriousness. "Sounds like distress I'd be sayin', I would."

"Stop kiddin', Big Joe," Skippy pleaded. "You mean you think it's *them?*"

"Well now I wouldn' be s'prised," the big fellow answered. Then seriously, he said: "We'll be gettin' there, kid! Don't be lookin' as if they was drownin' or somethin'. Sure they could keep afloat for hours so they could, and look at the tide besides."

Skippy glanced at the quietly rolling swell and felt somewhat reassured. But the voice of the siren jarred him and he was glad to see that Big Joe looked serious and determined. He hadn't liked that note of raillery in his friend's voice.

But despite Skippy's fears Tully answered the siren call with all the haste of a good Samaritan. One might have supposed that he gloried in the duties of heroic service. And when he reached the Channel and they sighted the distressed launch, he opened wide his throttle until the old hull shook to the vibrations of the engine.

Skippy clenched his slim, brown fingers and sat tense in his seat while a spray rained into the boat. Big Joe coughed significantly and drove his ramshackle craft straight for the disabled cruiser.

"Now ain't she the sweet lookin' baby," he observed as if he had never seen the launch before.

Skippy said nothing but grimly watched the three men who awaited their coming. Crosley he recognized at once, but the man standing alongside of him was a stranger. The third occupant of the *Minnehaha* was Marty Skinner. Skippy remembered him from his father's trial and from the night Skinner had ordered him off the *Apollyon* without a hearing.

"You see him?" he asked Big Joe between clenched teeth.

"'Tis all the better," Big Joe seemed to say in his bland smile.

He brought the kicker up alongside the *Minnehaha* and laid a life preserver over the coaming of his boat to prevent its scratching the gleaming hull of the launch. Skippy scrambled to the rescue and held the kicker as the ill-assorted pair rocked and rubbed in the heavy swell.

"Sure I don't want to be scratchin' her," said Tully with a fine assumption of humble respect for the launch. "I was tellin' the kid here, she's some baby, hey? What's bein' the matter; power give out did she? 'Tis too bad, so 'tis."

Skippy kept his eyes on space, but he had the feeling that Big Joe and he were being scrutinized with unfriendly stares.

Crosley sniffed the air contemptuously before he spoke.

"She's pumping oil to beat the band," he said. "We don't seem to be getting any compression either. We can't get a kick out of her. Been flopping around for an hour."

"Sure maybe ye be needin' new rings," said Tully. "Guess ye been pushin' her too hard, hey?"

He glanced into the cockpit and with a fine show of rueful astonishment, beheld the disastrous results of his own handiwork. She was indeed pumping oil. The engine head was covered with it, and it was streaming down the side over the carburetor. Three or four spark plugs had been taken out and lay on a locker in little puddles of oozy muck.

"If 't was only one cylinder now, I'd be sayin' ye had a busted ring, or even a cracked piston," Tully said blandly. "But shiverin' swordfish if it don't look like the whole six o' thim, don't it? Ye can't do nothin' here. Looks like ye was racin' her a lot." His detestable device had worked so well that he seemed moved to offer gratuitous suggestions. "I knowed a guy was stuck on the bar over by Inland Beach and he kept racin' his motor, and somehow—I dunno just how—she sucked in a lot o' beach sand and it sanded down his cylinder wall good an' plenty, so it did."

Skinner's lips were drawn in a thin line above his pointed chin.

"Does that mean we'll have to be towed back, Crosley?" he asked his host petulantly.

"Afraid so, Marty," answered Crosley. "I can't imagine how a fine engine like mine could break down so soon."

"Sure and if that ain't just like some guys," said Tully glibly. "They're fine's a fiddle one day and the next—they're done for, ain't it so?"

Crosley nodded indifferently.

"Could you tow us in?" he asked as if the question were distasteful. His aversion to the uncouth, but amiable river man was too obvious to escape Skippy's sensitive eyes.

If Tully was aware of it too, he did not betray it. His face looked grave and thoughtful.

"Trouble is I'm due at the Hook," he said hesitantly. "Have an all day's job towin' a barge. I'm late as 'tis. And if I ain't there in twinty minutes I lose the job, so I do. 'Tis the first good payin' job I've had in a long...."

Crosley waved his hand in entreaty.

"We'll see that you're paid for the loss of your day's job, man. How much would you get for it, eh?"

Tully moved his large head and shrugged his powerful shoulders. "Seventy-five bucks is what they're goin' to pay me," he said modestly.

Crosley gasped audibly.

"That's a lot of money, but...."

"It's a hold up!" snapped Skinner between his tightly drawn lips.

"Sure and it's what they're payin' me, boss," said Big Joe with a look of hurt pride. "I ain't askin' ye' for a cent, I'm not considerin' I may lose my customer for future jobs. 'Tis not only I'm losin' that seventy-five bucks, 'tis...."

"All right," Crosley sniffed angrily. "You're taking advantage of us. I don't believe you can earn seventy-five dollars for a day's work. But you have us at a disadvantage—the Lord knows who else we could get to our rescue in this unfrequented channel."

"So and that's all the thanks I get," said Tully. "Comin' way out o' me way...."

"All right," Skinner interposed. "Give it to him, Crosley. I know who this fellow is. We're at his mercy. But I'll remember this, Tully—you're occupying the mud banks at Brown's Basin. You and this boy, Dare, may want some consideration when you people have to get out of the Basin. And I'll remember who's living on the *Minnie M. Baxter*!"

"You oughta!" Skippy shouted angrily, rising to his feet. "Your cheatin' boss what's dead put it there, that's what, an' my father'll never see the sun on the river again on account of it too! So try an' take it away."

Skinner's cold dignity seemed unruffled. He averted his gaze while Crosley counted out seventy-five dollars to Big Joe Tully. Skippy stood by, his heart full of hate, and at that moment he thought that he could cheerfully see the *Minnehaha* sink to the bottom of the Channel while Skinner begged to be saved.

While leisurely chugging back toward the Basin that afternoon he and Tully talked it over seriously.

"Well, and we got seventy-five bucks aisy money out o' the tightwads," Tully chuckled in conclusion.

"Seventy-five bucks an' the promise of trouble from Skinner, Big Joe," Skippy reminded him with a note of apprehension in his voice.

Tully's face darkened.

"I hate Skinner for sayin' what he did, so I do," he said ominously. "Sufferin' swordfish if he do be makin' ye scared and drivin' ye outa the only home ye got—well, he better be lettin' ye 'lone. *Me*, I don't care much where I live, but *you* ... I'll be fixin' him if he...."

"Don't say it, Big Joe!" Skippy pleaded earnestly. "It scares me, 'cause that's just what Pop said the night he went to see old Mr. Flint on the *Apollyon*! It's sorta—"

"And 'tis all right, kid, so 'tis." Tully smiled. "Now ye be forgettin' it."

Skippy tried to; certainly he had forgotten that he himself had wished Marty Skinner a like fate only that morning.

***

CHAPTER XXV

DAVY JONES

Tully's game worked successfully for the next few weeks, for he had distributed his activities among various club houses dotting the shore. It had become an enterprise apparently without threat of untoward incident—so much so that Skippy, with his uncanny knack of presaging ill, came to feel that they must not go on with the distasteful business.

He had hated the treachery of it from the very beginning, partly because of his innate honesty and also because in fairness to himself, he knew he had no real grudge against his rich fellow men. And in his vague, ignorant way Skippy knew that Skinner and Crosley represented something which hate could never successfully combat.

He felt it particularly one early morning when Tully, swaggering out of the shanty of the *Minnie M. Baxter*, rubbed his large hands in gleeful anticipation of the next victim.

"'Tis up to the Riverview Yacht Club we'll be goin' this mornin', kid," he said confidently. "We've worked aroun' to it agin. Me pal, the boat tender what tipped me off on Crosley's *Minnehaha*, ain't there no more, but the new guy was aisy pickin'. He fell for a little split, without battin' an eye, so he did, and sent word down last night that a little fishin' party headed for Snug Island would push off at dawn."

"Snug Island, huh?" Skippy asked fearfully. "That means Watson's Channel for us again?"

"Sure," laughed Tully, "'tis a spot I like. Nobody goes through Watson's Channel 'cept they're headed for Snug Island. And nobody

                                          Among the River Pirates

goes to Snug Island fishin' but a coupla rich guys what own the whole place. It's aisy pickin' so 'tis."

"For you it's easy, Big Joe," said Skippy, "but not for me. Sometimes I think I never had anythin' so hard to do in my life as just gettin' up nerve to go on these trips. Gee, I ain't never had the heart to tell Pop about them—I lied, an' said we was makin' a pretty good livin' towin' an' fishin'."

Big Joe roared with laughter.

"Sure and we're towin' and fishin'," he said with a malicious wink. "Ye didn't tell Toby no lie. We fish the money out o' 'em and thin tow thim back—that's no story."

"I wish you wouldn't laugh about it, Big Joe," Skippy said with a frown. "It makes it seem as if it was a joke—as if you liked it almost."

"And you'd be likin' it too, kid, if ye wanted to get back at these rich guys much as I do. But I won't be laughin' about it no more, if it makes ye feel that way. Sufferin' swordfish but ye don't have to be actin' like we're goin' to a funeral."

"I feel funny about goin' to the Riverview Yacht Club this morning. Big Joe, would you stay away from there if I asked you to?"

"Any mornin' but this one, Skippy me boy," said Tully with all his old affection. "I can't be side-steppin' it on account o' this new boat tender. He's expectin' a little handout so I can't be disappointin' him. But I'll tell ye what, kid, if it's makin' ye feel so awful bad I'll chuck this game 'fore ye can say any more. I'll be thinkin' up somethin' else. Anythin' but seem' ye' feelin' sad, kid."

They got into the kicker and chugged out of the inlet once more. Skippy's eyes glistened happily and he told himself that he could forget the ominous whisperings inside of him for just this once. Indeed, he could forget everything distasteful in the past few weeks now that Tully had promised to give up the hated business.

"We ain't heard from Crosley or Skinner since that mornin' we towed 'em back, huh Big Joe?" he asked irrelevantly. "I wonder if they found out what was really wrong with the engine?"

"We'd o' heard 'bout it soon enough if they did, so we would," said Tully thoughtfully. "Anyways, I heard that Crosley sold the *Minnehaha* right that next day. He said he didn't want no boat that almost put him down in Watson's Channel. Ha, ha! Sure and I'm glad he did. He should be worryin' with his money."

Once more they pulled up beside the slip of the Riverview Yacht Club and once more Big Joe stole silently up the lawn in the gray morning shadows. Skippy waited patiently, albeit anxiously, and held the boat secure while his weary eyes blinked sleepily in the sultry air.

After a time, Big Joe came hurrying out of the shadows.

"Simple as sayin' meow, kid," he said exultantly. "The boat tender tells me this guy's goin' alone to Snug Island this mornin'. He couldn't be rememberin' the guy's name what owns her, but he says the boat ain't a week old. She's a peach—a trim, twenty-six footer, kid! And of all names she's got! Sufferin' swordfish!"

"What?"

"The *Davy Jones*—so 'tis. Can ye be beatin' that?"

"*Big Joe!*" Skippy said in a small, frightened voice. "That's a name that scares me terrible."

"*Ye're crazy, kid, ye're crazy!* Sure and what's in a name. Just 'cause Davy Jones happens to mean...."

"Just the same I'm scared terrible," Skippy maintained stoutly. "An' there's lots in names whether you believe it or not. Now take the *Minnie M. Baxter*—nothin' bad could come of her in the end, I bet, and if it did I bet it would be for the best, because it was my mother's name. Even if there's been trouble about the barge from the beginnin' there's good come on it too. When Pop was taken away, then you came to be good to me so that shows there's somethin' good about the barge, don't it? But Davy Jones only means one thing, Big Joe, an' you can say, what's in a name!"

What, indeed!

***

CHAPTER XXVI

THE ROCKS

It was a murky dawn and no sun followed in its wake. The air was heavy and oppressive, and low rumblings of thunder echoed in from sea. Skippy shook his head worriedly as they chugged out of sight of the bay to let the *Davy Jones* pass by.

"I don't feel right this morning, Big Joe," the boy insisted. "Say what you like, but we shouldn't wait—we oughta tail the *Davy Jones*, right away—*this minute*, before the storm comes on."

"Now ye be worryin' agin, hey?" Tully asked impatiently. "That storm's out at sea and it won't hit the Channel. Sure 'tis just a murky mornin'."

"All right," said Skippy, "but I know."

Tully was beginning to be annoyed with Skippy's gloomy predictions and he showed it. Yet somehow it gave him a little uneasiness and from time to time he glanced thoughtfully from the boy to the distant black horizon.

The storm clouds were coming nearer and thunder rolled ominously over their heads. Finally Tully turned over his motor and set her nose about. After she had warmed up, he opened wide the throttle and headed for the bay.

"I'll be keepin' her open and beat it for the Channel soon's we get across," he explained. "We'll be gettin' there sure 'fore the storm breaks bad."

"I hope so," said Skippy, "because it's travelin' in from sea, fast."

"We'll be goin' round by The Rocks and save fifteen minutes or so," Tully said hopefully searching the boy's face. "'Tis high enough tide for to take a chance."

The Rocks, that bane of all mariners who were unfamiliar with the lurking waters beyond the bay, could be safely passed in small boats at high tide. There were few, however, who took advantage of this concession of Nature to the small nautical man, nearly all mariners preferring the greater safety that was offered them by going the long way around Inland Beach.

A high wind was steadily rising as they chugged into the vicinity of The Rocks, and it prevented Skippy from hearing that call of distress for which he was so intently listening. Whether the wind was against them, he did not know, for the howling tempest and turbulent water drowned out all other sounds.

The storm broke after a few minutes and rain lashed at them from all sides. Tully said not a word, but stayed at his wheel silent and grave. And by his averted head, Skippy knew that he, too, was listening for that siren call from the *Davy Jones*.

Salt spray flung itself up over the bow and into Skippy's face. He could have moved farther back to avoid it, but he seemed incapable of action then, and sat tense and white, listening, listening....

Tully did not miss it. The boy's tragic expression so dismayed him that he felt for the first time in his life that he should have mended his ways while there was still time. All his sins seemed to have crowded into Skippy's face to accuse him.

And still they heard no call of distress from the *Davy Jones*.

Tully, desperate, raced his engine until they whistled through the foaming spray. Then suddenly they felt the keel grind under them with such force that it took all their combined strength to steady the boat and keep her from turning over.

"What happened, do you s'pose?" Skippy asked with white face.

"Sufferin' swordfish, kid!" Tully cried. "I think she's stove in—The Rocks! *Look!*"

   Among the River Pirates

He pointed and Skippy looked, to see a jagged hole in the bottom of the kicker. Water came in through it rapidly and even as he stared at it, it trickled over his feet and up to his ankles.

***

CHAPTER XXVII

SUSPENSE

"What'll we do?" Skippy cried. "Gee, what'll we do?"

"We'll be swimmin' for it, kid," Big Joe answered, his face ashen and drawn. "Inland Beach's nearest—we'll be swimmin' it in a half hour, takin' it aisy like."

"*Easy!* In this water and wind?"

"Skippy, don't be worryin'. Sure and I ain't goin' to see ye go down. I'll be keepin' ye up if it takes me life."

Suddenly Skippy turned, pleading. Big Joe knew and his eyes dropped before the boy's accusing gaze.

"And what can I be doin' about the *Davy Jones* now, kid!" he protested "I *got* ye to be thinkin' about now.... Sufferin' swordfish!" He groaned.

"Then we gotta swim to Inland Beach as fast as we can, Big Joe," Skippy said, master of himself once more. "We gotta get help right away for the *Davy Jones!*"

"Sure, sure," the big fellow moaned, "anythin', kid, only don't be lookin' at me so accusin'. Did I know it was goin' to happen like this? Sufferin' swordfish!"

"C'mon, Big Joe—*c'mon!*"

They had no sooner jumped clear of the boat than she sank out of sight. A terrific gale blew them along and Skippy kept close to Tully, buoyed up by the thought that he must keep going in order to get help for the *Davy Jones.*

Among the River Pirates

And for once Tully was right in a prediction. It took them all of the half hour before they sighted the sandy wastes of Inland Beach.

The summer colonists sheltered from the storm in their inadequately built bungalows sighted the bobbing heads of the swimmers as they battled their way against the tide. Speedily the beach was covered with people and the life-guards, summarily dragged from their bunks in their beach shanty, jumped drowsy-eyed into the life-boat and went into action.

Ten minutes later, the two were rushed up to the guards' shanty and hurriedly divested of their dripping garments.

"We gotta ..." Skippy began as soon as he had a chance to talk.

"We thought we heard a siren," Big Joe interposed. "Sure, it sounded like distress—there ain't a doubt."

"We heard it plain!" Skippy exclaimed anxiously. "An' it came from the Channel—didn't it, Big Joe, huh?"

"Sure and he's right. 'Tis about where I figgered she was comin' from," Tully added.

"An' we better start right out again!" Skippy said eagerly. "With this high wind...."

"A guy hasn't much chance in the Channel," interposed one of the guards bluntly. "I can tell you that before we start. And if it wasn't that you say you're sure you heard it, we wouldn't take a chance ourselves. Even a big tub like ours ain't a match for the Channel in a storm and high wind."

"But we're sure we heard it! Ain't we, Big Joe?"

"Sure we did that!" Tully said emphatically.

And so they started for the Channel.

The wind died down shortly after they had lost sight of Inland Beach. Presently the rain ceased and after a few moments' struggle with storm clouds, the sun came smiling through.

Skippy smiled too, hopeful that it augured well for the object of their search. Tully relaxed and took a cigarette that one of the guards offered him. He talked little and kept his eyes ahead.

They reached the Channel in a half hour and for a full hour they searched it up and down. Skippy kept his eyes on the water; he dared not let the guards see the hopelessness written there should his glance chance to meet Tully's.

"Sure we *couldn't* be dreamin' we heard a siren, now could we?" Tully pleaded when the guards announced their intention of returning to the beach.

"You guys didn't seem to be so sure you heard any at all when we first got you out of the water," one of the men reminded them.

"Sure and we were kind o' all in from the breaks we got," Tully explained. His voice sounded hollow and weary.

"Well, we don't hear no siren now," said the other guard, "and we've been up and down the Channel. If there *was* any guy in distress, maybe he's been swept out to sea. And we can't go hunting that far for you fellers. We'll send out word to the coast guard anyway when we get back just to be on the safe side. They'll find the tub if it's still afloat."

"An' if there was any siren signaling distress when that high wind first come up," said the first guard, "she's most likely screeching now for to get into Davy Jones' locker. Who knows?"

Skippy and Big Joe would have given their lives at that moment to know.

***

                                    Among the River Pirates

CHAPTER XXVIII

THE DUFFYS

They borrowed a kicker from one of the summer colonists and set out for home just before noon. Skippy was too overwhelmed to speak until long after they left the beach and Tully sat tragic and silent at the wheel.

"We might's well look agin," he murmured brokenly, as he headed the boat toward the Channel. "Just so's to be makin' sure."

"Might's well," Skippy echoed. Then: "Gee, do you think maybe he was blowin' the siren?"

"That he must o' done. He must o' been blowin' it like mad."

They spent half the afternoon chugging up and down the Channel and passed several craft, government and otherwise, which had heard the warning that the Inland Beach guards had passed along. Finally they decided to return home and with bowed heads found their way out of the treacherous waters.

"Sure if the coast guards ain't found him, we won't—not if we be stayin' there all night," said Tully mournfully. "Kid, don't ye be jumpin' on me, now. If ye knew what I been through since ... since.... I been blowin' a siren in distress five hun'erd times, so I have, and five hun'erd times, I been in that *Davy Jones* callin' me lungs out for help an' no help come! I've sunk with her too—oh shiverin' swordfish ... kid, I ain't nothin' but a plain...."

"Don't say it, Big Joe," said Skippy, moved to the depths of his soul with pity. "Gee, don't I know! You wouldn't have done it a-purpose."

"No. 'Tis right ye be there." Tully looked beaten.

They chugged on up the river and seemed to pass everyone they knew. Inspector Jones and his men bobbed by in the trim harbor launch waving a cheery greeting to Skippy and eyeing Tully with obvious suspicion.

Skippy was grateful for the silent inlet and the warm throaty bark that Mugs gave as he scrambled aboard the barge. He looked at the dog, winced a little at his faithful canine eyes and took him up in his arms. He couldn't do to Mugs what they had done to that unknown man on the *Davy Jones*.

He sprawled in a rickety arm chair on deck while the sun sank slowly in the west. The whole horizon was a blaze of scarlet, then gold, then purple and at last it faded into leaden colored clouds. Big Joe was calling him in to supper.

Skippy looked down in the crook of his arm at the sleeping dog. Supper? He didn't want any—he never wanted to eat while that man on the *Davy Jones* lay in Watson's Channel. He couldn't do it to Mugs.

Tully got tired of waiting and came out on deck. After one glance at Skippy's tragic face he got his hat, pulled it down over his head and left the barge while the boy watched him go with a constricted feeling in his throat. And though he wanted with all his heart to call Big Joe back, he knew that he could never again sit opposite him at the table with a dead man between them.

Dusk settled over the inlet and through the shadows came Mrs. Duffy. Her cheery smile was conspicuous by its absence just then and her cheeks looked tear-stained and haggard. Skippy forgot the dead man in the *Davy Jones*—he was all concern for this kindly neighbor who had helped nurse him back to health.

Hadn't Skippy heard? Mrs. Duffy sobbed a little, then bravely smiled through her tears. She had to be strong and brave—other wives and mothers in the Basin were getting used to the experience of seeing their menfolk taken in by the long arm of the law. And now Mr. Duffy had been added to that number.

What had he done? No more than other river folk had done before him. But it was forbidden by the law and there you were. And the excuse that they had to live and eat carried no weight in the courts of the land. Neither did the courts care that a rich and unscrupulous Josiah Flint had lured these men into his vicious employ at starvation wages only to leave them unwanted and ostracized from honest employment upon his untimely death. And Mr. Josephus Duffy, obeying that primal law of the survival of the fittest, was to be jailed for five years because he stole when employment was denied him. Five years of punishment for bringing food home to his family!

Skippy's young heart was bursting with sympathy. Wrapped up in his own and his father's concerns he had been vaguely conscious of his neighbors, the Duffys of the *Dinky O. Cross*. Squatters like himself, he had been aware that they came and went, but that was all. Now they became suddenly real and vivid to him—the Duffys, father and mother, and their two children, minus the father now.

"And wouldn't Skinner give him nothin' at the Central havin' two kids like you got?" he asked sympathetically.

"Skinner'd push men in prison before he'd help 'em get a decent job," the good woman said with a jerk of her head. "He said he's goin' to clean all us scum out of this Basin—ain't you heard?"

Yes, Skippy had heard only too well. He leaned over and timidly touched the woman's work-worn hands, pledging his slim, manly self as an aid and comfort to herself and her two unfortunate children. In gratitude, she hugged the boy to her breast and hurried back to the *Dinky O. Cross* to put her young ones to bed.

Skippy cherished that embrace; it was the only maternal affection he had ever known. His eyes shone into the darkness with the joy of it and he hugged Mugs still closer in his arms and spent some time in reflecting on why he was so happy when he was so sad.

Josiah Flint and Marty Skinner rose up before his eyes. He was beginning to realize what sorrow they had brought to the river people— *his people!* A fellow feels things like that when he's going on thirteen.

Thirteen! Skippy looked up into the starlit sky and blinked. Mugs' even breathing was like the whisper of the breeze blowing about his head. And he went to sleep planning how he could save the menfolk of the Basin from future prison life. He would see that the boys went to school as he himself had wanted to do so badly and he would see that they got decent, honest wages so that they could live as other people did in houses with pretty gardens....

Tully found him still asleep when he came back at midnight.

***

Among the River Pirates

CHAPTER XXIX

GOOD NEWS

"Skip—Skippy, kid!" Tully called, shaking the boy to arouse him.

Skippy sat up, startled. Mugs barked blatantly.

"What's up, huh? You look as if something'd happened—what's the matter?"

Tully motioned him into the shanty where he lighted the lamp and sat down.

"Can ye stand hearin' somethin' without faintin'?" he asked mirthlessly.

"I guess so," the boy answered shaking his straight hair from off his forehead. "But I hope it ain't anything worse!"

"Better and worse, sorta," Big Joe laughed ruefully. "But first so's to be aisin' ye, kid—the *Davy Jones* turned back, so she did, when she reached the bay this mornin'. From what the boat tender told me, sure must o' put a little extra dose o' the powder in the breather and she started kickin' up a rumpus a little sooner than ordinary, she did. So the owner, bein' a foxy guy, turned back when he heard that and saw the storm clouds comin' in from over the sea."

"So the *Davy Jones* ain't in her locker then, huh? Gee, am I glad!"

"Sure, and she got back to the club, and the owner had somebody come right away to be seein' what was wrong."

"Did they find out?"

"That they did, kid. He's got the police on the case, and I think they'll be workin' on me. But they ain't got no evidence so they ain't, and besides, I took all me powder and threw it in the inlet tonight, so I did."

Skippy sat down at the table, his head in his hands.

"Gee, I was afraid something awful would come of it."

"Now don't ye be worryin' too soon, kid. They'll have to be goin' some to get me.... You can bet on that."

"Gee, Big Joe, you don't savvy. It's the idea of gettin' the coppers suspectin' me and sayin' they expected sumpin' like that from Toby Dare's kid. That's what I couldn't bear Pop to hear after he's planned better things for me. Gee, I couldn't stand it!" Then: "Who owns the *Davy Jones*, Big Joe, huh?" he demanded.

"Now that's a funny thing," Tully said. "The *Davy Jones* is Crosley's. He bought her a week ago after he sold the *Minnehaha*. I s'pose that's why he played foxy whin the ingine wint wrong with the new one? If that big sap boat tender had only tole me who owned her I'd niver...."

"Gee whiz, Big Joe, now I can see why Pop said these crooked rackets don't pay in the end. It's account of that *if*. It's always if this or that didn't happen everythin' would be all right. But it never is. Oh, gee, I'm not hoppin' on you—maybe I'd been just like you if it wasn't that I'm sick and disgusted with crooked rackets already. Maybe it's because my mother came from a farm and so I'm not all river, huh? Anyway, I know I don't want any more of this business. I'm gonna be straight I am. I learned a lesson today on that *Davy Jones* business an' I mean it."

"Me, too!" said Big Joe with all his old time swagger. "I was tellin' meself comin' back here that if I think up an aisy racket where the coppers don't get wise, I'll be savin' up a few grand an' thin open up one o' thim hot dog stands in the country. Sure and the river won't see me at all, at all after that."

Skippy laughed outright—for, boy that he was, he could see that Tully would be Tully as long as the river flowed down to the sea.

***

                                                        Among the River Pirates

CHAPTER XXX

BEASELL

Next day, life in the Basin flowed once more in familiar channels. Tully trod the decks watching for the unwelcome police and puffing furiously on his cigarettes. Skippy sprawled in the rickety easy chair, playing with the dog and calling out to Mrs. Duffy some words of cheer when the occasion required. And when sunset came and the law had not put in its appearance they had supper noisily together.

Tully stretched out in his bunk after the meal had been cleared away. He looked at peace with the world. Skippy, watching him out of the corner of his eye, wondered what new racket he was planning now. And he didn't rest until he had asked the big fellow point blank.

"Me racket for a while, kid," Tully said amiably, "is to be keepin' ye from gettin' gloomy and sad. Whin I'm sure that Crosley ain't set the coppers on me trail thin I'll be turnin' around—see? Right now I'm stickin' close to the *Minnie M. Baxter*, so I be."

"And you could do worse, Big Joe, believe me. I'm gonna stick close too until I know what's what. But we'll talk about that then."

An insistent knock sounded on the door. Tully blanched and looked about for some means of escape. But Skippy, braving himself to the task, swung open the door to get it over with.

A man stood outside, bowing graciously and smiling. He stepped inside at Skippy's invitation.

"Beasell's the name, boys," he said. "Yuh heard how Marty Skinner's runnin' the works for Buck Flint?"

"Sure we been hearin' it too much, I'll be tellin' ye," Big Joe snapped as he came ponderously out of his bunk and stood on the floor.

"It's all jake then, big boy, you an' me won't waste no time," Beasell said unruffled.

"You've come to tell us...." Skippy began fearfully.

"Marty says all yuh squatters in this Basin'll have tuh scram by sundown tomorrow, get me? He's had all the rough stuff he's goin' for and that goes double for the warehouse guys. So it's scram in twenty-four hours, see? If yuh can't take these lousy scows out we'll blow 'em up, get me? Just a nice little Fourth uh July party, see?" He chuckled as if at a great joke.

"You can't blow up the *Minnie M. Baxter*!" Skippy cried. "Even a guy like Skinner can't take her from me 'cause, 'cause...."

"Lissen, punk, and you too, big boy, it's scram by sundown tomorrow," Beasell snarled. "Yuh better get me. I ain't kiddin' believe yuh me!" He scowled as he left to spread the bad news to the *Dinky O. Cross*.

"Sufferin' swordfish! Sure that Skinner's a lousy rat," Big Joe growled. "I should o' been pastin' that slimy Beasell but it wouldn't done no good. He's only carryin' out orders."

"Not only me'n you's gotta go, Big Joe," said Skippy plaintively, "but Mrs. Duffy an' her kids an' everybody here in the Basin. How're they all gonna pack up an' clear out by tomorrow night, huh? Gee, that ain't fair. There ain't one of us got a home to go to—gee whiz, these barges, why—they're home!"

Tully's face looked distorted as he walked to and fro across the shanty floor. Finally he turned.

"Sure Skinner don't know what it means to be sendin' that Beasell guy down here to be tellin' us we must be out by tomorrow night, bad cess to him."

"What d'ye mean, Big Joe?"

"Sure, folks here ain't like other folks, like ye've noticed. They been free for years and they ain't goin' to be kicked out without doin' some kickin' first thimselves. Law? Sure, they don't know what it's all about so what do they care, I'll be askin' ye."

Big Joe Tully had summed it all up in one sentence. They didn't know about the law, so what did they care about it?

It wasn't many hours before Skippy learned how little they did care.

***

CHAPTER XXXI

MOONLIGHT

Skippy waited until Tully was fast asleep that night, then he crept stealthily out of the shanty with the dog skipping and sniffing at his heels. He was careful to close the door softly behind him; he wanted to be alone.

It was a different Skippy that trod those decks, a new and older Skippy, who looked about the lumbering old barge through his father's eyes. It did not seem possible to him that Skinner could so ruthlessly order him away from the only home he had. Yet he realized that not many hours hence he would not even have *that* home.

He went forward and, getting to his knees, leaned far over and stared down at the trickling waters of the muddy inlet lapping against the hull. The dog, thinking him to be playing, jumped about with a soft whine to draw his master's attention.

Skippy tumbled him about for a while, then climbed down with him into the borrowed kicker that was anchored alongside the barge.

"We're gonna take one last cruise out and back in the inlet again—see, Mugs? I've just gotta see how the *Minnie M. Baxter's* gonna look when I think of her afterwards. I don't want to forget it's where I lived with two of the best pals I'll ever have, outside of Pop. Gee, Mugs, maybe it's silly to feel so over a barge," he confided to the attentive puppy, "but I gotta feel that it's sumpin' I must think a lot of. Every time I've visited Pop, he's asked me how was the *Minnie M. Baxter.* Just like as if she was a human being, he asked about her! So I love her on accounta my Pop. He's proud of her because she was so hard to get and because he decided to quit Ol' Flint and be honest so's I'd have a better chance."

                    Among the River Pirates

He started the kicker after this long confidence and steered it with one hand, putting his free arm about the dog. And as if cherishing the whispered confidences and affection, the animal cuddled close and remained perfectly still while the boat crept out to the mouth of the river.

As they turned back, a full moon broke through some dark clouds and shone brilliantly down upon the Basin. Skippy looked at the mellow, silver light gleaming over the grouped barges and he gazed in wonder at the fairyland that the moon made of the sordid colony. The dust at once became a shimmering film of silver and the washlines strung from shanty to forward deck contained fluttering bits of laundry that stirred flippantly in the soft night breeze.

Skippy's heartstrings tightened at the sight of it—he loved it all. His honest nature cried out against the injustice of turning all these people out of their homes. For that is just what it amounted to—no more and no less. Skinner knew that there wasn't a man in the Basin who could afford to have his barge lifted out of the mud. They would have to face it, he realized—they were people condemned!

He steered the boat farther on until he caught sight of the moonlight gleaming across his own shanty. Its shimmering rays picked out in bold relief the now dulled letters, *Minnie M. Baxter*, and he thought of a late afternoon when he and his father had looked on those same letters so new and shining, shining in the last brilliant rays of a dying sun.

He turned away from these reflections with heavy heart only to have his attention drawn to a boat, floating about the bow of the kicker. As he leaned forward to see it better, the dog growled ominously.

Skippy drew back instantly, gasping with horror. He sat stark still for a moment, as cold as ice and unable to take his eyes away from the battered face and body of a man he had seen in robust health but a few hours before.

That man was Beasell, Marty Skinner's lieutenant, and he appeared lifeless.

***

CHAPTER XXXII

THE LAST OF THE BASIN

Skippy was so frightened that he did nothing for a moment but sit and stare. Then suddenly he realized the terrible thing before his eyes, and he pulled the boat up alongside of the barge, trembling from head to foot.

The dog leaped out of his arms the moment he got on deck and refused to run with him to the shanty. But Skippy had neither the time nor the nerves to think of anything but the battered Beasell in the boat floating beside the barge.

He flung open the door of the shanty and rushed to Tully's bunk. The big fellow jumped up startled, and sat motionless while Skippy whispered of his discovery.

"Won't it go bad for everybody here?" he asked with agonized suspense. "Won't it, Big Joe?"

"Sure 'twill be just too bad, so 'twill," Tully said getting up and dressing. "Somewan did it what's gone cuckoo for thinkin' they'll be turned out o' their home tomorrow night. And crazy like, they beat up that Beasell thinkin' they'd be gettin' even with Marty Skinner—see? Sure I know me Brown's Basin, kid."

Skippy shivered with the horror of it. If Brown's Basin was like that, he wouldn't be sorry to leave it after all. Neither could he love people who used such ghastly means for their revenge against Skinner. He wanted to get away from it then, that minute.

"We gotta tell the police, Big Joe, huh?" he murmured.

Big Joe nodded as if he were dazed.

"Us river people ain't goin' to have no peace whilst Skinner's alive, kid!" he said in hard, even tones. "Whoever slugged that Beasell guy— well, *me*, I'd be goin' for Skinner, so I would. So he's goin' to take the *Minnie M. Baxter* from ye, is he? Well, we'll be seein' about that."

"Forget me for now, Big Joe. What worries me is, what're we gonna do with Beasell? Maybe he's dead."

"Now ye be goin' down and stay till I come, kid," said the big fellow, drawing on his shoes.

Skippy started for the kicker. He went forward but that was as far as he got for he became suddenly aware of a low, ominous rumbling noise that seemed to come from shore and run through the barge colony. Before he had a chance to determine what it was he felt himself lifted off his feet bodily and like a feather he was thrown into the muddy waters of the Basin.

There was a terrific detonation throughout Brown's Basin as Skippy came to the surface. Fire leaped from one barge to the other in the twinkling of an eye and the screams of men, women and children filled the turbid air.

Smoke poured skyward in great columns and in the light of the moon, Skippy saw the ponderous form of Big Joe Tully standing on the deck of the *Minnie M. Baxter* shouting and waving his hands. Suddenly he leaped into the kicker and the boy called out but he seemed not to hear in the din about them.

At that moment, the *Minnie M. Baxter* burst into flames. Big Joe Tully shouted deafeningly and Skippy, swimming hard to reach him, saw a strange, almost maniacal expression on his large face.

"'Tis Marty Skinner what's done this!" he was shouting to no one in particular. "'Tis him what's blowed this place up and took the kid away from me. 'Tis him! Skippy's dead—I'm sure he's dead! I can't find him!" he was almost whimpering.

"I'm here!" Skippy called frantically. "Big Joe...."

But Tully was even then steering the kicker out of the inlet. He had the throttle wide open and Skippy had no more than a glimpse of the racing craft before she slipped beyond his sight.

Logs, huge chunks of driftwood and every known article of household furniture, both broken and whole, floated in Skippy's path, blocking his progress. Suddenly he saw a little boat bearing down upon him, floating through the inlet unoccupied.

He reached out, grabbed the bow and climbed in, breathless and exhausted. Other kickers were shoving off filled with crying women and shouting men. Skippy looked about over the water, but saw nothing but a procession of slowly moving debris.

He turned over the motor and she responded with a fearful jerk. He was moving, in any event, moving away from the fearful heat that the burning barges threw out over the water. The moon's shimmering light now looked sickly and pale in contrast to the fearful red glare that spread over the entire sky.

The screaming sirens of motor boats soon became part of the pandemonium and Skippy heard commanding shouts for the boats to clear out of the inlet immediately. In the wake of this he heard a heart-rending shriek from the midst of the barge inferno which made him feel sick and weak.

"Mrs. Duffy an' her two kids ain't nowheres," a man's voice shouted above the roar. "I'll bet Skinner had that dynamite planted." And as Skippy attempted to turn the kicker about he was peremptorily ordered from the approaching police launch to keep on his way out to the river.

He didn't look back again. The *Minnie M. Baxter* was a seething mass behind him—there was nothing left. Big Joe was nowhere about— Skippy suddenly remembered the big fellow's shouts about Skinner. It gave him an idea and he nosed the boat down the river.

Out of this confusion of mind, he thought of the dog. He remembered then that he hadn't seen the puppy since he had let him down on the deck after seeing the battered Beasell.

Among the River Pirates

And what had become of him? Was he dead or alive? Skippy wiped a grimy hand across his forehead. He was utterly weary and exhausted by the ordeal. He could not think of an answer to anything. His world had toppled over since the discovery of Beasell and the explosion. And now Mugs was gone too—his skipping, faithful-eyed pal! Was there nothing left for him at all?

He put his hands over the wheel and gripped it bitterly, but soon he relaxed and with a soft sob he covered his face. And nobody knew but the river.

***

CHAPTER XXXIII

SKIPPY'S WISDOM

Skippy got the most out of his commandeered kicker. He opened it wide and raced her down the river and the closer he got to the bay the more apprehensive did he feel about Big Joe's flight. He tried not to attach any special significance to his good friend's shouts, but he could not help remembering Tully's earlier veiled threats about Skinner.

His fears grew as he chugged out into the bay and something urged him on still faster. Then he spied the glistening hull of the beautiful *Apollyon*, her anchor lights gleaming like stars against the night and a single light amidships.

Funny, the boy thought, how much it seemed like that night when he and his father had come for the showdown with the older Flint. Now there was to be no showdown, but he must warn Skinner against Big Joe's sudden maniacal fury. Queer that he should go to such trouble for a man who had given them no quarter in anything. But he was not thinking of doing Skinner a good turn beyond that it might prevent Big Joe from killing the Flint agent and being sent to jail.

He approached the yacht with his old feeling of awe. The deck was almost dark as he scrambled aboard but up forward he saw the rotund form of the second mate asleep and snoring in a luxurious swing. The boy could not help remember a very solemn resolve that night long ago, when the mate had sworn to be more faithful to his duties during his night watches.

With silent tread, he hurried along the deck and stopped before the lighted cabin amidships. Once, twice, he knocked softly, and waited.

Among the River Pirates

"Come in!" Marty Skinner's cold voice commanded.

Skippy stepped in, his heart bounding. He was thinking of the last time he had been in this room and closed the door, determined he would not be driven out again until he had had his say.

"Well?" Skinner snapped but this time he did not order Skippy out.

"You seen Big Joe Tully?" Skippy asked bravely. "He been here yet?"

"What d'ye mean—yet? I have no business with Tully and I haven't any with you that I know of."

"You're wrong both times Mister Skinner. 'Cause if you don't listen to me Big Joe'll be comin' here an' he'll try gettin' you an' he's so mad he'll probably kill you."

Skinner was all interest now. "He's mad and he may kill me and you come to warn me. That's funny."

"No it ain't funny. I wouldn't care much what happened to you Mister Skinner you been so hard on me'n Pop an' everybody, but I ain't gonna see Big Joe get in a jam an' maybe go to jail for life on accounta you. I'm tippin' you off so's Big Joe won't have no chance gettin' jammed. Maybe after that blowin' up of the barges tonight, which they say you ordered done, an' what happened to that guy Beasell I oughta let...."

"Blowing up barges? Beasell? What d'ye mean, boy? What happened?"

"Well, Beasell come an' ordered us outa the Basin by sundown tomorrow, sayin' it was your orders, an' if we can't get the barges out they'll be blowed up. Some time after he left me'n Joe I go for a boat ride. When I come back I see Beasell in a boat all battered an' lookin' as if he's dead. So I goes to call Joe an' while he's gettin' his shoes on I comes out again an' I just got near the rail when there's an explosion an' I'm tossed in the water. I swim till I find a boat an' climb in. I see Big Joe on deck an' he's yellin' that I'm lost an' acts like he's gonna get you when he jumps in his kicker an' races off without hearin' me. So I come right here to beat him to it an' keep him outa trouble, see?"

Skinner did not seem interested in the explosion. While he appeared callous as to the suffering and death that came in its wake he wanted to know more about Beasell. "D'ye think he's really dead?" he asked anxiously.

"Looked like that to me," answered Skippy, "an' if he wasn't he probably was blowed apart or burnt up." He wondered at the look of satisfaction that appeared on Skinner's face. "But you better be beatin' it Mister Skinner or Big Joe'll be here an' takin' you apart if he don't kill you."

"Well, if Big Joe comes here looking for trouble he'll get it—and plenty." Skinner reached under his left arm and pulling out a pistol laid it on the table before him.

Skippy heard footsteps and turned as if to shout a warning.

"Quiet you!" Skinner ordered as he picked up the pistol and leveled it at the door. Skippy with visions of his beloved Big Joe shot dead in his tracks as he opened the door wished from the bottom of his heart that he had not tried to warn Skinner. All he had done was bait the trap for Big Joe.

He stood there, a bit to the side of the desk, his knees shaking and, while his brain was active, he was so terror stricken that he could not open his mouth to warn Big Joe of his impending fate. He closed his eyes and said a little prayer as he heard the door creak a bit on its hinges. Why hadn't he left the door open when he came into Skinner's cabin, why....

A few tense seconds that seemed as so many hours to Skippy and then he heard the voice of Inspector Jones: "Now that's hardly the nice way to welcome a police officer, Mr. Skinner. I like your extended hand but not with a gun in it."

Skippy looked up to see Inspector Jones advancing into the room and this time a policeman's uniform was a most welcome sight to him. He breathed thanks that the visitor was not Big Joe.

"I'll just tuck the hardware away, Inspector, and give you the hand." Skinner smiled and did so. "I thought you were Big Joe Tully coming

   Among the River Pirates

in to get me. The boy here warned me Joe was on the warpath so I was all set to welcome him and beat him to the draw."

"So I could see," the Inspector commented. "Heard about the burning of the barges in the Basin and what happened to poor Beasell?"

"This boy told me there was an explosion and that some one slugged Beasell. Tell me is he—is he—dead?" The question sounded to Skippy as if Skinner was hoping the answer would be yes.

Inspector Jones looked sharply at Skinner. "Yes. He is," he answered simply and again looked up sharply as Skinner sighed as if in relief.

"Beasell was in my confidence. He knew my business and I trusted him," Skinner spoke as if to himself.

"Sure, I know you did," the Inspector agreed and there was that in his words which made Skippy feel as if there was something behind them.

"And how did you know that, may I ask, Inspector?" Skinner seemed a bit ill at ease.

"I talked to him before he died. We picked him up in a boat when we went to the fire. He had been badly beaten but before he died he regained consciousness. He talked plenty, too."

"What did he say? Tell who beat him up?" Skinner was plainly anxious.

"No, strange to say he didn't."

"Well then...?"

"Just this." Inspector Jones whipped out his gun. "Put 'em up Skinner and keep 'em up. I'm arresting you and I'm going to charge you with the murder of Josiah Flint."

"Why—why—that's—that's ridiculous, Inspector. You can't make a charge like that stand up on the ravings of a dying man."

"I didn't tell you that Beasell made any such charges. But I'm tellin' you now that he made a dying statement that he was in the kicker off the yacht when Skippy and his father came along, that he had been there some time, and hearing you and Flint quarreling, he watched through the porthole, saw you two struggling after Flint charged you with cheating him—saw you shoot the old man in the back when you twisted him around as he tried to snatch the gun you drew in your anger. He also saw you sit old Flint up again, scatter papers all over the place and take what money there was in his desk. Beasell's blackmailed you plenty since, threatening to turn you in."

"But—but——"

"And that isn't all," the Inspector went on relentlessly. "Buck Flint has been giving you a free hand and staying away, but he's had accountants working on your books and he's got plenty of evidence as to how you've ben cheating him and how you cheated the old man."

"No jury will ever convict me on evidence like that." Skinner seemed to have regained his composure. "Beasell was only a cheap crook anyway and he's dead, too. Stealing money isn't murder."

"Guess you're right on those points," the Inspector mused and Skinner started to lower his hands.

"Not so fast, not so fast there! Keep 'em up! There's one bet you overlooked, Skinner, and I'm going to call it right now." Still keeping Skinner covered the Inspector moved closer and pulled the gun out of the man's shoulder holster. "I've got a hunch that our ballistic expert will find a groove in the barrel of your gun which will prove the bullet which killed old Flint was fired by you. The gun never was found, you remember, but the bullet with a peculiar mark was and it's still right down at headquarters."

Skinner slumped into a chair at that, but Skippy looked quickly from his dejected figure as he heard a familiar bark. He turned to the door and there in the arms of a policeman was his beloved Mugs.

"Mugs! Mugs!" he cried out overjoyed. And then, as if in afterthought, "See anythin' of Big Joe, officer? Gee, if he'd only come along now, 'cause I know my Pop's gonna be free soon, everythin'd be just grand. Gee, but I'm happy. I'm...."

He stopped suddenly frightened at something he saw in the policeman's face. "What—what—what's wrong? Tell me," he demanded.

                                    Among the River Pirates

"I'm in a tough spot, kid, but I know you got plenty guts, so here goes point blank. Big Joe went back to your barge figgering you might have found your way back there. We see him and tell him you're safe. Then he hears the dog barkin', goes into the flames after him and saves him." He paused, gulped, then went on: "He was burned bad, Big Joe was. Fulla smoke, too. Well, anyways ... he kicked off."

There was a silence, which was finally broken by Skippy's sobs. At a motion from Inspector Jones the policeman, who had brought Mugs and the sad news about Big Joe, handcuffed Skinner and took him out of the cabin, softly closing the door.

It was far in the night before Inspector Jones had Skippy sufficiently comforted so that the boy fell asleep. Then the Inspector bundled him up, carried him to the police launch and that night Skippy and Mugs slept at the Inspector's home.

***

CHAPTER XXXIV

THE GREAT ADVENTURE

Skippy had two things to show his delighted father when they met at the railroad station a few weeks later, by which time Skinner had confessed murdering Josiah Flint when mad with rage at having been caught stealing, and Skippy's grief over Big Joe's death had become less poignant. One was the gawky Mugs and the other a little satchel which he carried under his arm with the greatest care.

"What's in there, Skippy son?" Toby asked after their outstretched arms had clung in an awkward embrace.

Skippy winked at his father mysteriously.

"I waited to tell you now, Pop—sort of as a surprise. It's what Buck Flint calls redress money—money that Old Flint should have paid you and didn't. And he says it's for the price of the *Minnie M. Baxter* too. Altogether he said he figured Old Flint owed you a thousand dollars with interest—see Pop?"

Toby was overwhelmed.

"What we a-goin' ter do with it, son?" he wanted to know.

"Whatever you say, Pop. There's enough to buy another *Minnie M. Baxter* and more besides, huh? An' there's enough to buy a nice hot dog stand somewheres up in the mountains where the doctor said I wouldn't have no more bad throats. So what do you say, Pop?"

"Mountains, Skippy boy," said Toby with shining eyes. "We'll call our stand the *Minnie Baxter* jest the same, hey? 'Cause didn't she sort uv bring us luck in the end, after all? How'd we got all this money if she

                                    Among the River Pirates

hadn't uv burned up and that helped ter show up Skinner and made Buck Flint feel sorry and that he ought ter make good. Yessir we'll call her that."

A train announcer sauntered out of the big iron gates and in his sonorous voice called out, "Mountain Express on Track Number Four ... Cold Glen ... Pine Ridge ... Baxter...."

"Did yer hear that, Skippy?" asked Toby excitedly. "There's a place in them mountains what's called *Baxter*! Seems like as if it was Fate or somethin'! S'pose we jest try her fer luck. What do you say?"

"I'm on, Pop," Skippy cried joyfully. "Baxter for luck!"

And arm in arm, Skippy and Toby, with Mugs sniffing at their heels, darted through the big iron gates on their Great Adventure.

THE END.